Secret Love

He was still angry at himself. What a prize fool. Cindy must have seen how he was feeling. She must have seen the longing in his eyes. He had been kidding himself when he thought she felt the same. He remembered saying he would show her this place, now she'd never trust him enough to come with him. And if she told Carl... He didn't really want to think about it. One thing he was sure of, though, he had fallen in love ... *really* in love for the first time in his life. But that love had to be a secret ... for now ... probably for ever.

Also in the Point Romance series

Look out for:

Dream Ticket: *Blazing Kisses*
Amber Vane

Malibu Summer
Jane Claypool Miner

Point Romance

Secret Love

Sue Welford

■ SCHOLASTIC

Scholastic Children's Books
Commonwealth House, 1–19 New Oxford Street,
London WC1A 1NU, UK
a division of Scholastic Ltd
London ~ New York ~ Toronto ~ Sydney ~ Auckland

First published by Scholastic Ltd, 1996

Copyright © Sue Welford, 1996

ISBN 0 590 13480 9

Typeset by TW Typesetting, Midsomer Norton, Avon

Printed by Cox & Wyman Ltd, Reading, Berks.

All rights reserved

10 9 8 7 6 5 4 3 2

1

Drew's first sight of Cindy Raven hit him like a bolt from the blue. He was in the college car park with his best friend, Skip, when he saw her. They had just got there on Drew's motorbike. Drew had taken off his crash helmet and was combing back his shock of thick, dark brown hair with his fingertips.

Skip must have noticed her at the same time because he rolled his eyes and gave a low whistle. "Who's *that*?"

Drew was still standing with his mouth half open, staring at her. Her close-fitting denims and white shirt might have looked ordinary on anyone else. But on this girl they looked a million dollars. There was something about the way she moved, the way she tossed back her mane of pale hair, that made Drew's breath catch in his throat. She must have been just about the most gorgeous girl he'd ever seen. The man she was talking to was pointing in the direction of the Business Studies department. Drew saw a flash of silver from her earrings as the girl nodded her thanks. Then, with a wave of her hand she hitched her bag up on her shoulder and made off in the direction of the west wing.

Drew had the sudden, incredible urge to run after her. To find out who she was, where she came from. He must be going off his head.

Skip was saying something else. "I've never seen her before. I reckon she must be new."

Drew tore his eyes away. He put his helmet in the box at the back of his bike and locked it up. He looked over again at the place where the girl had been standing. "Yes," he said in a dreamy voice. "She must be."

"You ever seen her before?" Skip asked.

Drew could only shake his head. "No ... never," he murmured.

"Well, once seen, never forgotten," Skip glanced at his watch. "Come on, Old Tucker will go barmy if we're late first day back."

"Right." Drew blinked and came back to reality. It really wasn't any good fantasizing about a girl like that. Girls doing Business Studies *never* mixed with boys from Engineering, everyone knew that. Anyway, it was pretty obvious this girl had class, real class. Those expensive-looking clothes, her hair, her golden tan. Even her white plimsolls looked as if they came out of a fashion magazine. Certainly a girl like her would never look at a guy with Drew Devlin's background. A house on a council estate, a mum struggling to make ends meet, a father in prison for fraud ... no way!

The two friends hurried round to the Engineering block. They were both in the second year of their Mechanical Engineering course.

Mr Tucker, their instructor, known to everyone as Old Tucker, was standing by the workshop door. "Ah, Devlin and Smith," he said, making them sound like a comedy duo. "Last in as usual."

"Sorry, sir," said Skip, the class clown, as he made a mock salute. The boys ran up the stairs two at a time and took their seats in class.

Drew was glad when lunch-time came. He hadn't been able to concentrate on his work all morning. He had changed the plugs on a Ford Escort twice before he realized they hadn't needed changing in the first place. Actually, he was supposed to be doing something else entirely, but he couldn't think what. All he could think about was the girl he had seen earlier on. He couldn't get the picture of her out of his head. It was no good, he *had* to find out who she was.

In the canteen, he caught sight of her again. He was just taking a bite of his cheese sandwich when she came through the door. She was with a crowd of other girls. They collected trays and went up to the counter. Drew's eyes followed her every move. She selected a can of Diet Coke and a couple of tuna sandwiches. She handed over her money to the cashier then stood by the till gazing round for somewhere to sit.

"Hey, Cindy, over here," someone called.

Drew's heart thudded. So that was her name. It suited her. He would have felt strangely disappointed if she had been called something like Ann or Elizabeth. Somehow, Cindy was just right.

Just at that moment, Skip spotted her too. She was heading their way. "Look, there's that girl again! She's really something, isn't she?" he said, excitedly.

Drew nudged him. "Hey, keep your voice down. She'll hear."

Drew stared at Cindy as she came towards them. She held her tray up high to avoid colliding with people on the way. She had a loose, easy way of walking. A certain grace that belonged to people who'd had ballet lessons as a child. She was quite tall and slender as a willow.

Her face broke into a smile as she got near Drew's table. She seemed to be looking straight at him. She had the widest, deep blue eyes he had ever seen. Her face was tanned, no make-up apart from a touch of pale lipstick. She was even more gorgeous than he'd thought.

Drew felt heat coming to his face. He couldn't just sit there staring at her with his mouth open. She would think he was nuts. He lowered his head quickly and took a bite of his sandwich.

When he looked up, Cindy had gone right past. He caught a whiff of her perfume. Light. Flowery. A smell that reminded him of summer. She had sat down behind him. She hadn't been smiling at him at all but at someone on the next table. He felt a bit of a fool and hoped she hadn't seen him staring at her. The more he thought about it, the more he doubted if she had even noticed him sitting there at all, going red like a complete idiot.

In fact, he really hoped she hadn't noticed him.

He heard her say "thanks" as someone pulled a chair out for her.

Drew sighed. His heart was still thudding like mad. He ran his hand round his jaw. He wouldn't have known what to say to her anyway. He would have just stammered something dumb like he always did in these situations. He'd been out with several girls but none of the relationships had lasted long. He just didn't know what to say to them and that was that. In fact, Drew was a pretty shy kind of guy. He'd always thought of himself as a bit of a loner, never one to follow the crowd. He was a lot happier messing around with car engines or working out at the gym than he was with girls.

Skip was giving him a knowing grin. "What's up?"

"Nothing," Drew mumbled. He screwed up his sandwich wrapper and crushed his Coke can in his hand.

"Yes, there is." Skip looked at him shrewdly. "It's that girl, you fancy her." He pushed his baseball cap to the back of his head. His spiky black hair popped out from underneath as if it was on springs. "I'll tell her if you like."

Skip reckoned if you wanted something you should go for it, no messing.

Drew was more cautious. He usually thought about things a lot before he did them. He glowered at Skip from beneath his dark eyebrows. "Don't you dare."

Skip grinned. "Just kidding. If you fancy her, why don't you ask her out?"

Drew shook his head. "She'd hardly look at *me*, would she?"

Skip shrugged. "Oh, I don't know. You're not a bad looking guy." His friend eyed him up and down. "Tall ... pretty good muscles. All that working out obviously does something other than make you sweat. Then there's those sexy brown eyes..."

Drew burst out laughing. "Come off it."

"Well, my sister fancies you."

Drew snorted, still grinning. "Yeah, but she's only sixteen."

"True." Skip grinned back. "But have you seen her recently?"

"Saw her last week round at your place."

"Yes, but have you seen her when she's dolled up to go out?"

Drew shrugged. "No, what of it?"

"I reckon you'd be surprised," Skip said.

Drew couldn't imagine it somehow. OK, Marie was sixteen but he could still only see her as that scrawny kid with freckles and glasses. He remembered he used to tease her about them all the time.

"Anyway," Skip was saying, "that bike of yours gives you a certain –"

"Smell of oil?" Drew raised his eyebrows. He spread his hand in front of him. "Greasy fingernails?"

"No, girls like motorbikes. They think they're macho."

"Well, I haven't exactly noticed them queuing up."

"No ... well..." Skip shrugged. "You never know your luck. You could be just the guy she's been waiting for."

Drew thought it was doubtful. He was a pretty good judge. Somehow he didn't think *this* girl would consider his motorbike at all macho. By the look of her, some guy with loads of money and a flash sports car might be more her type. And as he didn't have either, or was ever likely to have, he reckoned he may as well forget he'd ever set eyes on her.

But Drew couldn't forget her. All through the day he went about in a dream. He just couldn't get her out of his mind. It really wasn't like him at all. If he had seen a picture of a gleaming Harley in a bike magazine and kept thinking about that ... now that would be different. But a girl ... a girl who didn't even know he existed. He must be going mad.

Old Tucker got really annoyed.

"Devlin, if you can't do better than this you're not going to get through your last year, you know," he complained. He had to repeat a question three times before Drew realized the lecturer was speaking to him.

Drew did his best to pull himself together after that. No one was more relieved than he was when the day was finally over.

He gave Skip a lift home.

"You off to work later?" asked Skip, as he climbed off Drew's bike outside his front gate. Skip's house was just round the corner from

Drew's. He put Drew's spare helmet in the bike's carrier and snapped the lid shut.

"Yep, 'fraid so," Drew said. He worked at the Pavilion Hotel at weekends and a few evenings after college during the week.

The Pavilion was the newest and most sumptuous hotel in the area. It was situated a little way out of town and had been converted from a small stately home. It used to be well outside the built-up areas but a huge new housing estate had almost filled the land between. It still had magnificent gardens that led down to the river. There was a newly built leisure and fitness centre attached to the main building, with a gym, sauna and solarium together with a swimming pool. It had become the favourite venue for the town's wealthy business people and their families.

Drew's job was to clean up around the hotel car parks and generally do any odd jobs that needed doing. He didn't like the work much but the pay wasn't bad and they were flexible about his working hours. The one good thing about it was that Drew got to work out at the gym for free. Max Lewis, the instructor, was a pal of his. Staff weren't normally allowed to use the hotel's facilities. Not unless they paid like everyone else. There was no way Drew could afford that kind of luxury.

Spots of rain fell on Drew's head as he rode into the hotel grounds that evening. He had been home, grabbed a quick meal, then headed back through town towards the hotel.

He rode past a gleaming pale yellow Rolls Royce

parked by the main entrance. The limousine belonged to the owner of the hotel, wealthy entrepreneur, John Hickson. Up the top of the front steps a shining glass door was flanked by a pair of marble pillars. The door had "Pavilion Hotel" emblazoned in gold letters on the front.

Drew rode round to the staff car park, tucked away at the back. He got off and squinted up at the darkening sky. He unbuckled his helmet. They were in for a lot of rain by the looks of it. "That's all I need," he muttered to himself. Hopefully, the boss would take pity on him and find him a job indoors. It was no fun sweeping up the car parks and weeding the flower borders at the best of times, let alone in the pouring rain.

The swing doors of the staff entrance banged together as Drew went through. He unzipped his jacket and walked along the corridor, whistling. He was still thinking about Cindy. She had got to be the best looking girl around. He sighed. Good looks, classy clothes ... they didn't mean a thing really. He'd rather have someone with a brain and a good personality. Maybe she had those as well. He sighed again. Who was he kidding anyway? She'd never go out with him in a million years.

Drew usually thought of himself as a pretty determined type of guy. If he wanted something badly enough, he generally went all out to get it. He'd saved for well over a year to buy his bike, religiously putting away what money he had left by the time he'd paid his mum for his keep and bought his books for college. He'd made up his mind not to let the fact that his dad was in prison change his life either. That had been really hard. Luckily, the trial had taken place in a different town so the news hadn't been in the local paper. The neighbours knew about it, of course. And Skip and a few other guys Drew had been at school with when it happened. And he guessed his college tutors knew as well but if they did, they had the decency not to mention it. But Cindy...? He may as well forget it. It was obvious she was way out of his league and that was that.

"Hey, Drew!" Max Lewis's loud voice came booming along the corridor.

Drew turned to see the gym manager swaying towards him. Two metres tall, muscles like iron, the huge West Indian was just about the biggest guy Drew had ever set eyes on. He'd been a professional body-builder in his day. Not only did Max have a big body, he had a great heart as well. He always found time to listen to Drew's troubles. Drew waited by the locker room door.

Max grinned broadly. "How's it goin', Drew?"

Drew gave a wry smile. "OK, I guess."

"You workin' out tonight?"

"If that's OK," Drew said.

"Sure is," said Max.

Drew usually finished around nine, depending on how much work there was to do. That would give him plenty of time for a good work-out before Max closed the place up. "Great," he said. "See you later then, Max."

Max slapped him on the shoulder, almost making him lose his balance. "See you later."

Drew's boss, head caretaker Jim Appleby, was in

the locker room. He was studying the work rota. "Ah, Andrew. Just the person I wanted to see." Drew smiled to himself. He had never once arrived at work without Jim Appleby saying that to him. He put his jacket and helmet into his locker. He took out the bright green overalls with Pavilion Hotel embroidered on the breast pocket. Drew hated those overalls more than anything else he could think of. He climbed into them and straight away felt ridiculous. It was the colour more than anything. He didn't mind the dark blue of his workshop overalls but these green ones were a different kettle of fish altogether.

"Right," Mr Appleby eyed him over the top of his spectacles. He made a mark on his list. "Window cleaning this evening, Andrew. Mr Hickson's been on the war-path. He said the covered way into the fitness centre's filthy. Your job, I'm afraid."

Great, Drew thought, just my idea of heaven, cleaning windows. But if he wanted to carry on with his course, he'd got to do it. Part-time jobs were hard to come by and he'd be a fool to chuck it in. His mum had trouble making ends meet as it was. And with his sister, Soph, still at school and the rent going up in leaps and bounds, things were pretty tight.

Mr Appleby was tutting impatiently. "Well, get on with it, Andrew. You know where the stuff is."

"Yes, Mr Appleby."

Drew made a face and zipped up his overalls. He took his green hotel baseball cap out of the pocket and put it on his head with a sigh of resignation.

*   *   *

Drew was up the step ladder polishing the last section of overhead glass when he saw her. Cindy. She was coming out of the gym with Carl Hickson, the hotel owner's son. She was wearing a pink leotard with navy blue Lycra cycling shorts. Her tanned legs looked fantastic against the spotless white of her Reeboks. Her corn-silk hair was tied up on top of her head with a twist of bright blue cotton. Her face was shiny, flushed from working out. Her eyes were glowing. In fact, she looked so gorgeous, Drew almost fell off his ladder gazing at her.

His heart sank right to his feet when he saw who she was with. Carl Hickson of all people. Drew had been at school with Carl and they had never seen eye to eye. Hickson was the type of guy who thought he was better than everyone else. He reckoned just because he had muscles, good looks and a rich father, the girls would fall at his feet. As far as he was concerned, things like personality didn't come into it. The trouble was, girls *did* fall at his feet. And here he was with the gorgeous Cindy, as if to prove it.

Hickson was tall. Taller even than Drew. He had a chin that looked like it was carved out of rock, shoulders like a quarter-back and blond hair cut in the latest fashion. He wore the most expensive track suit money could buy and carried a real leather sports bag. He looked like something out of a health and fitness magazine. And Cindy, with her arm through his, seemed like his perfect partner. Together, they looked like an advert for one of those exercise machines that claim to give you the perfect body.

Hickson caught sight of his reflection in the newly polished glass and stopped to run his hand through his hair. Drew felt slightly sick. The guy was so vain it wasn't true. He had always been the same. Even at school he had spent half his time looking at himself in the mirror, the other half chatting up good-looking girls.

Drew pulled his baseball cap down over his eyes. He rubbed frantically at an imaginary spot on the glass. With a bit of luck he hoped Carl wouldn't see him – although he did have a horrible, sinking feeling he knew just what was going to happen. Hickson had never forgotten the time Drew had come across him bullying one of the younger school kids. Drew had landed him a punch that sent him flying. He always reckoned Carl was just waiting to get his own back. Every time they met there was a grudge simmering just beneath the surface. Today was no exception.

"Why, it's old Devlin."

Drew looked down to see Carl resting his hand on the side of the step ladder. He pushed his cap back so he could see better. Chill out, Devlin, he thought. He might give the impression he was a pretty laid-back sort of guy but he did have a temper. And the person most likely to make him lose it happened to be standing underneath his ladder right now.

"Carl," Drew said lightly. "Fancy seeing you."

The truth was, Drew often saw Carl around the hotel but usually managed to avoid him. The last thing he wanted was Carl to hand out his usual snide remarks in front of Drew's work-mates.

Behind Carl, Cindy was fiddling with her hair. She gazed briefly at Drew, then looked away. It was obvious she thought he was just another hotel worker in a stupid green overall. Which he was, of course. Drew realized he had been harbouring a vain hope that Cindy just might recognize him from college and maybe say "hi" or something. It would at least mean she had noticed him, if nothing else.

Gazing at her, Drew reckoned he'd been right. Looks she definitely had. And a great figure. But if she was going out with a guy like Carl Hickson she couldn't have much of a brain – that was for sure. As for Carl ... well, Drew knew there was nothing he liked better than having a good looking girl on his arm. He'd been out with almost every pretty girl in the area. To him, brains didn't mean a thing.

"What's new then, Devlin?" Carl said. "Still up to your old tricks?"

Drew looked down. He decided that was the best place to be, looking down on Carl Hickson. Cindy had gone on towards the door into the hotel and stood waiting patiently. "What tricks are those then?" he said coolly.

"The kind of tricks your dad gets up to," Hickson said. Drew felt a warm flush of anger. Hickson was one of the people who knew about his father and if they did get into conversation, he never failed to mention it.

"Very funny." Drew turned back to his polishing.

Carl went on gazing up at Drew. "Well next time you visit him he'll teach you one or two," he said, grinning. "You could end up polishing prison windows instead."

This was too much for Drew. He shot down the ladder. Hickson certainly had the knack of making him lose his temper without barely trying. Drew stood in front of Carl, his chest heaving. The urge to punch him in the face was almost too strong to resist. Seeing him on the deck with a fat lip again might almost be worth losing his job for. Drew's fists were clenched by his sides.

"Touch me and you're out of a job, Devlin," Carl said, smoothly.

"It would be worth it," Drew said, angrily. Even as he said it, he realized it wasn't true. He needed this job desperately and Hickson knew it.

"Yes? Why don't you try it then?" taunted Hickson. Drew tore his eyes away from Carl's grinning face. Common sense told him it *wouldn't* be worth it. He glanced at Cindy. She was staring at them with alarm on her face. Carl gave him one more look then went off to catch her up. She spoke to him and he answered, glancing back at Drew then saying something else. Drew watched them go through the swing doors into the hotel. He took a deep breath and went back up the ladder. There was no doubt about it, if Drew had another run-in with Hickson he'd get him fired and that was the last thing he needed. There was no guarantee he'd find another job, that was for sure.

"Haven't you finished yet, Andrew?" Mr Appleby came marching along the corridor. "I've got several other jobs lined up for you before you knock off."

"Sorry," Drew mumbled. "Almost done." He began to polish away like mad. He was annoyed to find his hand was shaking. But whether it was shaking with anger or with excitement because, for one brief moment, the beautiful Cindy had been so close to him that he could see the intense blue of her eyes, he really didn't know.

It was almost nine o'clock before Drew had finished his chores for the evening. It was windy outside. The twilight stars were hidden by heavy rain clouds.

He got his things from his locker and went through to the gym. He was still smarting from his encounter with Carl. He really didn't know why he was letting it get to him. It really didn't matter *what* someone like Hickson thought of him. But somehow, having to put up with his sarcasm with his girlfriend there was just too much. Drew sighed. Maybe she hadn't heard, although Hickson had a loud booming voice that could probably be heard all over the building. He sighed again. A good work-out was just what he needed to get him back on an even keel.

Max was behind the reception desk. He was reading a body-building magazine. Loud rock music thumped from the video screen up on the wall.

The gym was almost empty. A couple of middle-aged men were heaving a few weights around. A red-faced woman pedalled furiously on one of the exercise bikes as if she was doing the Tour de France.

"Hi, Drew. How's things?" Max asked as he came through the door.

Drew sat down on a stool and leaned his chin on his hands. "Rotten, if you really want to know."

Max closed his magazine. He took a can of low calorie drink from the cold cabinet. He handed it to Drew.

Drew shook his head. "Sorry, no dosh."

"Have it on me," Max insisted. "What's up? It's not like you to be fed up."

Max was another one who knew about Drew's dad.

"Carl Hickson's been winding me up, that's all." Drew told him what had happened.

"Don't let him bother you," Max said. "You're worth ten of him."

Drew snorted. "Thanks for the vote of confidence." He took a swig from the can. "Who's his girlfriend anyway, any idea?"

Max's face split in a broad grin. "She's only the daughter of John Hickson's new business partner, that's all. Carl made a point of tellin' me just who she was. Their parents have known each other for years apparently. She's been livin' in Australia for a while and they've just come back and settled in this neck of the woods."

"Australia?" Drew raised his eyebrows. That accounted for the sun-tan. He'd wondered where she'd got it. "What kind of a business partner is her dad?" he asked.

"Property developer," Max replied. "They're plannin' to build one of those forest holiday centres … you know, the ones that are all built under

glass. Pools, restaurants, fitness centre ... the lot."
He rolled his eyes. "I reckon it'll cost millions."

"Must be loaded then."

"I guess so," Max said with a grin.

"And she's going out with Hickson," Drew said almost to himself. "I saw her at college today," he added. "I thought she was really something else."

Max must have heard Drew's wistful tone. He shook his head. "Believe me, Drew, you'd be wastin' your time."

It was as if Max could read his mind.

Drew finished his drink and got off the stool. "Tell me about it," he grinned. He felt better already. "OK if I use the machines now?"

"Sure, go ahead. Hey, I need to leave a bit early. Can I leave you to lock up for me?"

"Be glad to," Drew said. He often helped Max around the place in return for his free work-outs.

Everyone else had gone by now and when Max left, Drew had the place to himself. He turned the music up loud. There was nothing he liked more than lifting the weights, working his muscles hard. The music pounding to the rhythm of his heart. Only tonight it wasn't quite like that. Drew couldn't get Cindy off his mind however hard he worked. She was still there, in front of him, her long lashes sweeping her cheeks, her pale hair drifting over her shoulders like corn-silk.

"You're crazy, Dev," he said aloud. "Plain crazy."

But it was no good. The image just would not go away.

*　　*　　*

It was raining really hard by the time Drew finished. The wind had dropped and the air was muggy with the threat of thunder. He showered quickly, dressed and put on his leather jacket and crash helmet. Then he switched all the lights off and locked up.

The water thumped down on the glass dome of the covered way as Drew went through to hand the key and the cash tin to the night porter. The plush scarlet and cream hotel foyer was deserted. He handed them over, said goodnight and left.

The car park was awash. The lights from the hotel reflected in the puddles like a rainbow world beneath their surface. Drew had just lowered his visor when he noticed someone under the lamp in the corner. Visitors to the fitness centre often used the staff car park as it was closer than the one reserved for the hotel's guests. The figure was crouched down trying to undo one of the wheel nuts on a Mini.

Thinking they might appreciate a hand, Drew strode across.

He lifted his visor. "Need any help?"

A figure in a navy track suit, wet hair plastered to her head, gazed up at him. "Oh, yes please!"

Drew froze. It was Cindy. He could hardly believe his eyes. Why hadn't she gone home with Hickson? Surely he hadn't left her out here in the pouring rain to change the wheel by herself?

Cindy stood up and leaned one elbow on the roof of the car. She pushed back her dripping hair. "I've been out here for ages trying to get the wretched nuts undone. I was just about to give up and go and phone my dad."

Drew took the wheel brace from her hand. "Sit in the car if you like. I'll do it."

Cindy shook her head and wiped drops of moisture from her eyes. "No, if you'd just loosen them for me I can do the rest."

Drew shrugged. "OK." He was grateful for his crash helmet. It covered the flush that had come to his cheeks when he'd realized who she was. He took the brace from her hand and crouched down by the wheel.

Suddenly a bolt of lightning ripped across the sky, followed by the boom of distant thunder. Cindy flinched. Drew looked up. "Get in the car if you're scared."

He could see she *was* frightened but determined not to show it.

"It's OK," she insisted. She glanced anxiously at the sky again. "It won't take long will it?"

"No." Drew gritted his teeth and heaved at one of the stubborn wheel nuts. It suddenly gave way. "Be done in a tick."

Cindy watched him. She glanced overhead every now and then. "I feel a real idiot," she said. Drew looked up to see her staring down at him. "It's no good me working out several times a week if I haven't got enough muscle to undo a few measly wheel nuts." He noticed her voice had a very faint Australian twang to it.

"There's a bit of a knack to it really." Drew stayed kneeling and heaved off the wheel.

20

Lightning flashed again. Another clap of thunder split the air then grumbled away into the distance.

Cindy ran round to the boot to get the spare. Together they put it on. She held it steady, her shoulder leaning against Drew's as he tightened up the nuts. He lowered the car jack. "There you are," he said. "Bob's your uncle."

Cindy slammed the boot. She looked wetter than ever. Her track suit top clung to her like a second skin. Her hair hung in rat's tails around her face. Drew saw her shiver and then hug herself for warmth. He opened the car door.

"You'd better get home before you get pneumonia," he said softly.

Cindy held out her hand. When he took it, it felt small and fragile and it rested in his as if it belonged there. He swallowed, shook her hand quickly then let it drop.

"Thanks so much," she said. "I'm really grateful."

"No problem," Drew said.

He stood by the door as Cindy got into the driving seat. She looked up at him. "My boyfriend will be really upset when he finds out," she said. "He didn't know if he could make it or not tonight so we came in our own cars. His was parked round the front so we said goodnight inside. He'd have helped me if he'd known."

"I'm sure he would," Drew said.

"Are you staying at the hotel?" Cindy asked. It was obvious she hadn't recognized him as he was wearing his bike helmet. Either that or she had forgotten seeing him up a ladder polishing glass just a short while earlier.

Drew shook his head. "I work here part-time. I go to Westbrook College."

"Oh, that's funny. I go there too."

"Yeah?" Drew hoped he sounded surprised.

Cindy pulled a face. "I'm doing boring old Business Studies. What are you doing?"

"Mechanics," he said.

"Lucky you. I'd like to have done that. My parents wouldn't let me. They thought I was crazy but I've always wanted to know how cars and things work."

"I'll lend you some books if you like."

Cindy's eyes lit up. "That would be excellent. Look, I'm sorry … you're getting soaked."

"I could meet you tomorrow lunch-time and give them to you," Drew said quickly, surprising himself. He didn't care *how* wet he was getting. He would have stood there talking to her all night if she let him. "Would that be OK?"

"That would be brilliant. Where? What time?"

"Twelve-thirty … in the canteen?"

"Great." Then her face fell and she shook her head. "No, er … perhaps not. Hey, maybe I could come over to the engineering block?"

"OK, I'll meet you by the workshop entrance."

"Right," she said. "One-thirty, is that OK?"

"Great. See you then."

"Thanks again," she said. "You're my knight in shining leather."

"In wet leather you mean," he said grinning.

Cindy beamed him a brilliant smile through the rain spattered window. At the entrance to the car park, she hooted the horn and flashed her headlights before roaring off down the road.

Drew stood and watched the car's red tail lamps disappearing into the distance. He gave a whoop of joy. He jumped two feet off the ground, then ran back to his bike.

Exactly what Cindy would say when she realized her knight in shining leather was Drew Devlin of window cleaning fame, he had no idea.

But whatever it was, he just couldn't wait to find out!

2

Drew stood by the entrance to the Engineering workshop. He glanced anxiously at his watch. It was almost one-thirty the following day. He'd been there for almost half an hour already. He had hoped Cindy would be early and they could spend some time chatting before going back to classes.

It was a lovely day. Last night's storm had washed the pavements clean. Everything seemed new and sparkling. In one of the trees a blackbird sang. Its sweet notes tumbled in the warmth of the spring sunshine.

Drew walked up and down for a while then perched on the low wall that surrounded the college grounds. He took his books from under his arm and put them on his lap. He glanced at his watch again. Exactly one-thirty. Any minute now he'd see Cindy coming round from the other side of the campus. Would she be wearing those great denims again, and that white shirt she looked so good in? He grinned to himself. Even last evening, soaking wet, she'd been the best looking girl he'd ever seen. What a pity she already had a boyfriend. And what a pity it was Carl Hickson! Anyway, as he told himself before, even if she *wasn't* going out with anyone, she'd hardly look at someone like him.

Drew glanced up to see Skip standing beside him.

"What are you hanging around for?" his friend asked. "We're supposed to be in Room Three."

Drew gazed up at Skip through his shaggy fringe. He combed it back with his fingers. Then he looked at his watch again. It was almost quarter-to-two. It didn't look as if Cindy was coming after all. He stood up and glanced in the direction of the Business Studies block. "You go on, Skip," he said. "I'm supposed to be meeting someone."

"OK, see you later." Skip went through the swing doors. Drew heard him running up the stairs. "Come *on*, Cindy," he said to himself, quietly.

Then, at two o'clock he gave up. It was obvious she wasn't going to show. She must have got held up. He sighed. What a waste of time. He had been thinking about her a lot, sitting there, waiting. She had seemed so sweet and friendly last evening. One of the few girls he'd met who had great looks and a good personality to go with them. What he couldn't figure out was why she was going out with someone like Hickson.

Drew pushed through the doors and ran up the stairs. She probably had a good excuse, but even so he hated being let down. He had a face like thunder as he banged his way into Room Three. She could at least have sent someone across with a message to say she couldn't come.

He flung himself down in a chair and gazed moodily out of the window. He ignored the curious stares of his class mates.

Skip turned in his seat. "Didn't they show up?"

"No. I guess she had better things to do."

"She?"

"Cindy," Drew said.

Skip's eyebrows shot up. He leaned his elbows on the back of the chair. "Cindy?" he said incredulously. "You had a date with Cindy?"

Drew frowned, then grinned. "Not a date, idiot. I just promised to lend her some books, that's all."

"Oh." Skip turned back to face the blackboard. "Is that all. Well, I suppose beggars can't be choosers."

Drew leaned forward and punched him playfully on the shoulder. "Thanks very much. With friends like you, who needs enemies?"

Drew found himself staring out of the window almost all of the afternoon. The lecturer's voice droned on and on but he really didn't have a clue what the woman was on about. He made an effort to scribble a few notes about catalytic converters but they didn't seem to make any sense. He really didn't know why he should feel so upset that Cindy hadn't turned up. The truth was, she had probably merely forgotten. She was just being polite last night, just grateful because he'd helped her out. She may not have had any intention of really meeting him at all.

He had just packed the books into his carrier bag and buckled on his helmet for the ride home after lectures when Skip nudged his arm. "Hey, here she comes."

He looked up to see Cindy hurrying towards them. She looked stunning in a pair of tight black jeans and a white T-shirt. She arrived a bit out of breath.

She nodded to Skip then smiled at Drew. Gold earrings like little bells swung as she tossed back a lock of hair that had fallen over her eyes. A fine gold chain glowed against the tanned skin of her neck. For the first time he noticed she had a small mole on her left cheek.

"Look, I'm really sorry about lunch-time," she said to Drew. "I got held up. I hope you didn't hang around too long."

"Only about three hours," Drew said.

Cindy pulled a wry face. "I'm really sorry."

Drew grinned. "Only kidding. I guessed you couldn't make it."

Cindy looked relieved. "Thank goodness for that."

Behind Drew, Skip cleared his throat. "Well, see you, old buddy," he said.

Drew raised his hand. "Right, see you tomorrow."

"Bye," Cindy flashed Skip a smile as he pedalled off on his mountain bike. She looked back at Drew. "Could I take the books now?"

"Sure," Drew rummaged about in his carrier bag and came up with them. "They're pretty basic stuff."

Cindy's fingers brushed his as she took them from him. Drew was surprised to feel a kind of electric shock shoot through his body. He breathed in sharply.

She obviously hadn't noticed and was thumbing through one of the books. "They're great," she looked up at him. "Thanks. Actually, my car's given up the ghost. I think all that rain yesterday was too much for it. It spluttered all the way home last night then wouldn't start at all this morning. I got a lift to college with my boyfriend."

"Yeah?" Drew raised his eyebrows. "I could take a look at it for you if you like."

"Hey, that would be great. Would you charge much? I have to pay for stuff like that out of my allowance."

Drew shrugged. "I wouldn't charge anything, only for new parts if you needed any. I quite often do friends' cars for them."

Her eyes shone. "Well ... if you wouldn't mind. It's sitting in the drive looking sorry for itself at the moment. My dad could do it but he never gets a spare minute. Look..." She sought around in her bag and came up with a notebook. She wrote something down, tore off a page and handed it to him. "My number," she said. "Give me a buzz when you can come round."

"Right." Drew took the piece of paper and shoved it into the back pocket of his jeans. He felt as if he was in a daze. Cindy had given him her phone number! Then he came back to reality. Her car had conked out. He was the guy to mend it. The fact that she had given him her number meant nothing. It was purely a business arrangement. He was kidding himself if he thought it was anything more.

He swallowed. "I'm pretty busy in the evenings but I'll give you a buzz at the weekend if that's OK?" That's better, he thought. That sounds cool. As if I don't really care one way or another. It was a good job she wasn't standing that close to him though. She might have heard his heart thumping, as if he had just run a marathon.

"Great." She beamed him another of her dazzling smiles. She waved the books at him. "And thanks for these. If I read up on engines, maybe I could help?"

"Sure." Drew grinned back at her. He tipped the bike forward off its stand and swung his leg over the saddle. "There's no hurry for them back, it's stuff I did last year."

"Right." Cindy was gazing at him. "Hey," she said suddenly. "I don't even know your name."

Drew was just about to tell her when an open-topped sports car came roaring up and parked on the other side of the road. Carl sat at the wheel, wearing a pair of dark glasses. He looked like a movie star. He sat for a moment with his elbow resting on the edge of the open window.

Cindy waved to him then turned back to Drew. "There's my boyfriend, I'd better go."

"See you, then," Drew said.

She smiled. "Yes."

Drew watched her get into the car. She leaned across and kissed Carl on the cheek. He saw her show him the books and glance at Drew. Carl looked his way, too. Drew could see he was frowning. Then he said something else to Cindy, put the car into gear and roared off down the road.

Drew sighed, switched on the ignition and headed off home.

Drew's mother was in the kitchen as he came in. He put his jacket round the back of a chair and dumped his helmet on the table.

Mary Devlin was tall and slender like her son, with light brown hair and blue eyes. Drew had got his dark good looks from his father.

Mrs Devlin was just getting her coat on ready to go out to work. She was a nurse at the local hospital and looked tired from a week's night shift.

"Good day?" she asked, as Drew got a Coke from the fridge, pulled the tab and took a swig. He sat down.

"Yes, thanks…" Then he thought about all the time he'd spent hanging around for Cindy and her not turning up. "Well … OK, I suppose."

"You don't sound too sure."

He told her what had happened.

"It doesn't sound as if it was her fault," his mum said.

"No, it was just a bit of a waste of time, that's all."

She patted his arm. "Never mind." She picked up her bag. "I must go, I've got to stop off at the supermarket before I go to work."

"I could have done the shopping," Drew said.

She shook her head. "It's OK, I've got to get stuff

for Sophie's cookery lesson, it's a bit complicated."

"I could still have done it."

Mrs Devlin kissed the top of Drew's head. "Yes, I know. But it's all right, really."

Drew frowned. "Couldn't Soph have got her own stuff?"

Mrs Devlin sighed. "She's having tea over at Joanne's. Anyway I've got to do some shopping for us, a bit extra won't hurt."

"You're a real mug, Mum, you know that?" Drew said angrily. His sister, Sophie, was just about the most selfish person he'd ever met. His mum had enough to do without having to run around after her as if she was still a little kid.

"Tell me about it," his mum said with a weary smile.

Drew caught her hand. "You look tired, Mum. Get Soph to do her own shopping next time, huh?" He made up his mind to have a word with his sister when she came in.

"Now don't go on at her, Drew. She still misses her dad, you know."

"She's not the only one." Drew looked past his mother and gazed out of the window.

His mother put her hand on his shoulder. "I know. Look, Drew, I must go or I'll miss the bus. See you in the morning."

She went out and shut the door quietly behind her. Drew saw her hurrying down the path and along the road to the bus stop. Things were tough enough for her without having to run around after Sophie all the time. He would definitely have a word with his little sister when she came in.

*   *   *

Just as Drew was getting his tea, the phone rang. It was Skip.

"How did you get on with the body beautiful?"

Drew laughed. "What do you mean, how did I get on with her? I was just lending her some books that's all."

"Oh." Skip sounded disappointed. "I thought maybe you'd ask her out."

"You're nuts," Drew said. "Anyway she's got a boyfriend. Carl Hickson."

Drew heard Skip snort down the phone. "Hickson! Trust him to have all the luck."

"Exactly," Drew said.

"So you're not going to see her again?"

Drew explained about the car. "She gave me her phone number," he said.

"Her phone number?" Skip put on a silly voice. "She must be attracted to you then."

"Don't be daft ... I told you she's going out with Hickson ... she'd hardly ditch him for me, would she?"

"No, but she must think you're OK, all the same," Skip said.

Drew ran his hand through his hair and leaned against the door frame. "Skip, you're fantasizing."

"I'm not, you know. Think about it, Drew. She doesn't need you to get her car going. By the looks of her, her family's loaded. She could easily take it to a garage."

Drew explained about her allowance.

"You wait," Skip said wisely. "I know about these things."

Drew laughed again and hung up.

He thought about what Skip said as he munched his way through two helpings of spaghetti bolognese. Even if Cindy's parents were rich it didn't mean they handed everything to her on a plate. If they did then she wouldn't be driving around in a clapped-out Mini in the first place, would she?

He was still thinking about it as he got ready for work. He was just about to leave when his sister came in. He knew she'd arrived because the front door banged hard enough to break the glass.

"That you, Soph?" Drew came out of the bathroom and called down the stairs.

"Who do you think it is, Snow White?"

Sophie had the knack of always answering one question with another. She stood in the hall taking off the black cape she'd got from the Oxfam shop. When she arrived home with it a week or two before, Drew had told her she looked like Dracula's daughter. She'd given him one of her witch looks and stormed off up the stairs in her black DMs and mauve mini-skirt.

Sophie barged through into the front room and slammed that door, too. Drew heard one of her Heavy Metal tapes blaring out. The neighbours would be banging on the wall before long.

He finished shaving and put on his best jeans and sweatshirt. He didn't really know why he was putting on his best stuff. He didn't usually dress up to go to work. He supposed, in the back of his mind, that if he happened to see Cindy he wanted to be wearing something decent. When she did eventually find out what he looked like beneath his bike helmet he wanted to look his best. He stared at himself in the mirror. He turned sideways and flexed his muscles. He supposed he wasn't *that* bad looking. Not hunky like Carl of course, but then who was? Then he realized he was being pretty silly anyway. Even if he did bump into her she'd hardly take much notice of him. Especially if she was with Carl and especially if he happened to be wearing his grotty green overalls. He could tell by the way she had looked at Carl when he saw them together that she thought he was the best thing since sliced bread.

Drew poked his head round the front room door to speak to his sister before he left. "You going to be OK on your own?"

Sophie sat with her feet up on the settee chewing a lock of her hair. She didn't look at him. "What do you think?"

"I think you should have some company if possible while I'm out." Drew said patiently.

"Judy's coming round, isn't she?" Sophie mumbled.

Judy was Sophie's friend from two doors down. Drew's sister might be pretty disagreeable around the house but he reckoned she must have some charms. She had more friends than anyone else he knew.

"Well, don't raid the fridge."

"If I do you won't be here to stop me will you?" Sophie made a face without looking at him.

Drew went in and sat on the arm of the sofa. "Why don't you cheer up for a change, Sophie?" He was going to mention the shopping but Sophie looked unhappy enough without upsetting her even more. Drew was like that, always trying to spare people's feelings if he could.

"I'm perfectly cheerful," Sophie scowled. She jumped off the sofa and switched off the cassette player. She swept past him and ran up the stairs. He heard her bedroom door bang.

He shook his head, rose and went out.

It was such a balmy evening that Drew decided to walk to work. He loved walking along by the river. His favourite place of all was just along from the road bridge. It was a place he and his dad had discovered years ago. If you went down the bridge steps and over the stile you could walk along the river into town. Half-way along there was a disused boat-house in a narrow man-made creek. It was hidden by rampant hedges and great weeping willows that grew over the entrance. No one had used it for years. You could push your way through and sit by the willow trees on a spring day and watch kingfishers feeding their young along the banks of the inlet. Or gaze at swans gliding past as if they had all the time in the world. He often went there for a bit of peace and quiet, if he wanted to study, or read in the sun or just sit and think for a while.

There was no time to linger this evening though. If he didn't get a move on, he'd be late for work. He strode along the footpath, up over the lock gates and made his way through the riverside gardens to the Pavilion Hotel.

As he crossed the car park Drew noticed Carl's

car by the entrance to the fitness centre. Maybe he'd give his work-out a miss that evening. He just wasn't in the mood for sparring with Hickson tonight.

The car was still there when Drew finished work. On his way to the locker room, he spotted Max talking to one of the porters in the corridor.

"Comin' for your work-out?" Max called as he saw Drew walking towards them. He nodded goodnight to the porter.

"Thought I'd give it a miss tonight," Drew said.

"You've gotta keep at it if you want to look like me," Max grinned and flexed his forearm.

Drew grinned back. He'd never get as big as Max in a hundred years. "Well, man, I'll keep trying," he joked. Then his face fell. "Truth is I didn't want to see Carl tonight. If he's in one of his sarcastic moods I just might smack him in the mouth."

"You won't have to," Max said. "He's not here."

Drew frowned. "His car's outside."

Max shook his head. "Well, I haven't seen him all evenin'. He must be doin' something else."

"OK," Drew said, changing his mind. "I might just see you, then."

Max slapped him on the back. "Good man. I've told you before, you don't want to let him get to you."

Drew pulled a face. "I keep trying."

In the locker room Drew took off his overalls, grabbed his sports bag and made his way through to the gym.

Loud rock music hit him as he went inside. The place had almost emptied out as it usually did this time of the evening. In one of the mirrors Drew could see the reflection of a blonde girl lying on one of the benches pumping iron. He drew in his breath. He'd recognize those tanned legs anywhere. Cindy.

Max had appeared and was grinning at him from behind the counter. "Stop starin', Drew. You can be arrested for those thoughts you're havin'."

Drew hadn't realized he was gazing at her so intently. He scratched his cheek. "Who, me?"

Max grinned again. "Yes, you. If I was twenty years younger I'd be havin' them myself."

Just then, Cindy came over to get a drink from the cold cabinet. She was wearing pale pink cycling shorts with a faded black T-shirt that said "Bondai Beach" on the front.

"Thanks, Max." Cindy handed him a fifty pence piece. She pulled the tab and took a swig from the can. She wiped her face on the sweatband around her wrist. She nodded to Drew.

"Hi," she said, frowning slightly.

He swallowed quickly. "Hi." His voice sounded husky so he cleared his throat noisily. He glanced at her face then looked away.

Cindy was regarding him with a puzzled look in her eyes. One dark blonde eyebrow creased in a slight frown.

"You know Drew Devlin?" Max said, by way of an introduction. "Drew, this is Cindy Raven."

"Hi," Drew said again. He was thinking what a crazy surname for someone so blonde as Cindy. He dropped his eyes, suddenly too shy to return her curious gaze.

Someone called Max from across the gym to go and adjust one of the machines. He left the counter. Cindy was still staring at Drew. She narrowed her eyes slightly then took another drink from her can.

"I saw you the other evening, didn't I?" she said. "You had a bit of an argument with Carl."

So she had noticed him after all. Drew scratched one eyebrow. "Er ... yeah. We go back a long way, me and him."

"Oh? He didn't say."

Drew shrugged. "No reason why he should."

"No, I suppose not." She was still looking at him as if there was something about him she couldn't quite make out.

"How were the books?" he said lightly.

A ghost of a puzzled smile crossed Cindy's generous mouth. "Books?"

"Yeah," Drew said. He smiled. "Car mechanics..."

Cindy hesitated then her face broke into a broad grin. She slapped her hand to her forehead. "Of course! I knew I knew you. You're my knight in shining leather."

"Window cleaning's not my only talent you know."

Cindy laughed loudly. "I don't believe it." Her eyes sparkled. She looked Drew up and down and he was so glad he'd worn his best clobber he could have jumped for joy.

"Wet leather I should have said." She was still smiling.

He put his hand to his chest and grinned. "That's me."

"I'm sorry," she said. "I just didn't tie you up with…"

"With the guy in the yukky green overalls cleaning windows?"

"Er … well … to be honest, no I didn't."

He could see she was embarrassed. "It really doesn't matter," he said quickly.

She took a deep breath. "The books are great … a bit complicated."

"It's better when you're actually working on an engine," Drew said. He leaned against the counter and tried to look relaxed although his heart was thudding. "You know, the diagrams and stuff actually mean something."

Cindy was still smiling and shaking her head. "You know I've been thinking about you. I really wondered what you looked like underneath your bike helmet."

She had been thinking about *him*? Drew's heart leapt. This could be his lucky day.

She seemed to have forgotten all about the car manuals and was still staring at him, a curious mixture of pleasure and disbelief on her face.

He spread his hands. "I know, I know. Don't tell me. Now you've found out, you think maybe I should keep my helmet on all the time?"

Cindy laughed although her eyes were serious as they washed over his face. "No … no … you're better without it."

"Thanks very much."

Their eyes held and locked. For a brief moment it seemed to Drew that time itself had stopped. The music, the thud of the weights, the whir of the exercise bike … they all faded into nothingness. Cindy's bright eyes were staring at him. She had a wide smile on her mouth … the mouth he suddenly realized he wanted to kiss so much it was threatening to drive him crazy.

Suddenly he had to sit down. It was stupid but his knees were shaking like jelly.

She lowered her gaze. "Well…" She finished her drink and threw the can into the bin. "I'd better warm down." She glanced up at the clock. "I've booked a sauna."

"Right," Drew said.

She smiled. "See you, then. Let me know when you can come round to look at my car."

"Right, then. I'll give you a buzz."

She glanced at him over her shoulder then got on the rowing machine. She began rowing as if her life depended on it. Drew got up from his stool and went into the changing room.

When he came out, Cindy had gone.

Drew had finished his work-out, showered and said goodbye to Max when he saw her again. He was just making his way out of the car park. He was beginning to wish he'd come on his bike after all. A long walk home in the dark suddenly didn't seem such a great idea.

A car drew up beside him. He glanced round. "Oh, no, Hickson," he said to himself. "That's all I need."

The door of the yellow convertible sports car opened and a voice called out. "Want a lift?"

To Drew's complete amazement, it was Cindy.

He leaned down, one elbow on the open door. "You've bought a new car," he joked. "You couldn't wait for me to ring … you women are really impatient."

Cindy laughed. "You know it's Carl's. Do you want a lift or not?"

Drew slung his sports bag into the back and folded himself into the front seat. He shut the door and fixed his seat-belt.

He looked at her and grinned. "Yes, please." He wanted to add *wild horses wouldn't stop me*, but thought better of it.

"Which way do we need to go?" She put the car into gear.

"Left at the roundabout."

There was a screech of tyres as they roared off. Drew clutched the side of the cream leather seat. It looked as if Cindy was as mad a driver as her boyfriend. Drew had met him on the bypass once, overtaking the bike at over eighty miles an hour. He glanced sideways at her. She'd swapped her shorts and T-shirt for a white mini-skirt and denim jacket, although she still wore her spotless trainers. He wondered what Carl would say if he knew his girlfriend was giving him a lift home. He felt a sudden pang of jealousy. Sports car, a girlfriend like Cindy … some guys had all the luck.

"Where is Carl tonight, then?" Drew asked, curious to know why she was on her own.

"He's pulled a muscle in his back so he's having a night off from training."

"Oh dear," Drew said, unable to help the sarcasm in his voice. She glanced quickly at him, then looked back at the road. "So he lent you his car?" Drew added. "Pretty generous of him."

Cindy didn't comment. "Where's your motorbike?" she asked instead.

"I walked," Drew told her. "I came along the river. It's—" He broke off. She probably wasn't the slightest bit interested. She'd probably think he was a wally anyway if he started going on about wildlife and stuff.

"It's what?" she asked gently.

He shrugged. "It's beautiful. Peaceful … away from the madding crowd, you know? There's a place I know where you can sit all on your own and no one knows you're there."

She glanced at him, frowning slightly. He could see she was puzzled. Maybe she'd only known boys like Hickson who thought caring about that kind of stuff made you a freak.

"I like places like that, too," she said. "Whereabouts is it?"

Drew told her.

"Sounds lovely," she said.

"Yes," Drew said. Perhaps she didn't think he was a wally after all. "Maybe I could show you some time."

"That would be great. We lived in the city in Australia and there never seemed to be anywhere really quiet to go. Not just on your doorstep, anyway."

"What's it like?" he asked. "Living in Australia?"

"Great, most of the time," Cindy said. "Brilliantly hot in summer, of course. Sydney is wonderful. You ever been there?"

42

Drew laughed. He'd never even been to France, let alone Australia. "Me?" he said. "No chance."

She glanced at him again. "You never know ... you might one day."

"Well ... maybe," he said. His real dream was to go to the States but he didn't think she'd want to hear about that.

She drove along in silence for a minute or two. Drew couldn't help thinking what it would be like to sit by the river on a summer's day with Cindy beside him. He decided it would be the closest thing to heaven he could possibly imagine. Not that there was any likelihood it would ever happen, but there was no harm in dreaming.

"Whereabouts do you live?" she enquired.

Drew was miles away. "Huh?" he said.

She grinned. "I said where do you live? I could be going in absolutely the wrong direction."

"Um ... no ... you're OK." Drew hesitated. He didn't really know why but there was no way he wanted Cindy to see the estate. It wouldn't have been so bad if the bloke next door hadn't decided to dismantle a lorry in his front garden and leave it there for nine months. Or if the local kids didn't chuck their drinks cans and crisp packets all over the pavement on their way home from school. He wasn't exactly ashamed of the place. It was just that he didn't want to her to see it, and that was that.

"Er ... Eastmead," he said at last. Maybe as she was new in town she wouldn't have heard of the estate's reputation. "But you can drop me by the railway bridge ... it's not far to walk."

"It's OK," she said, flashing her lights at a car that had just overtaken them, going too fast. "I'll take you right to your door." She gave a cheeky grin. "I'm making the most of this car while I've got the chance."

"Don't blame you," Drew said.

"I know," Cindy said suddenly. She leaned over the steering wheel and shifted her position. "Let's go for a spin. You don't have to get home yet do you?"

Drew thought about Sophie alone in the house. Her friend would probably have gone home by now. He really should get back.

"I'd really like to," he said. "But my sister's on her own. I'd better get home."

"Oh, OK." Cindy sounded disappointed.

"Some other time, maybe," Drew said, surprising himself.

"I doubt it, somehow," said Cindy. "Carl only lent his car to me because his dad heard mine had conked out and told him he had to. He's not actually generous where his car's concerned."

Drew almost said he'd thought it was too good to be true but resisted the urge. It would be no good running Carl down to Cindy, she was obviously crazy about him. Her voice went kind of dreamy when she was speaking about him. Drew couldn't really think why. In his experience, Hickson was more likely to give you nightmares.

Drew stared out at the passing shop fronts. They were almost at the end of the high street by now and had skirted the industrial estate and sports centre.

"How old's your sister?" Cindy asked.

"Fourteen," said Drew. "And don't I know it."

Cindy smiled. "I bet she's not as bad as *my* sister. She's thirteen going on twenty-five."

Drew laughed. "I know what you mean."

"Mind you," Cindy went on. She pushed her hair back with her hand and leaned forward to wipe mist off the windscreen. "I was pretty awful at fourteen … weren't you?"

"No." Drew shook his head and smiled. "I was absolutely excellent. A model brat."

Cindy glanced at him again then grinned broadly. "I bet." She was apparently getting used to his sense of humour. They had reached the cross-roads. "Which way now?"

Drew breathed a sigh. She evidently didn't have a clue where Eastmead was. "Left," he said. "Then as far as the fire station. You can drop me on the corner if you like."

But when they got there she insisted on taking him right to his door. He tried to argue but it was no good. He came to the conclusion that Cindy was a pretty determined lady. At least it was dark and you couldn't see his road properly. Half the street lamps were out anyway, so the place didn't look so bad.

"Here," he said, when they reached his gate.

The light was still on in the front room so Drew guessed Sophie must be up watching some totally unsuitable late movie. He turned to get his bag from the back.

"Thanks," he said.

"You're welcome."

He hesitated. "Would this weekend be OK?"

"To look at my car ... yes, it would be great. If you're not doing anything else."

"Saturday?"

"Yes, great."

"It'll have to be in the morning, I'm at work in the afternoon."

"That's fine."

Drew suddenly realized he didn't know where she lived. He climbed out of the car. He leaned on the open door and put his head inside. "It might help if I knew where your house was," he said.

She laughed. "Yes, I suppose it might. Manorfields," she said. "Number three ... the house is called 'Spindrift', do you know where it is?"

"Yes." Drew knew all right. He might have guessed Cindy lived in the poshest area of town. "I'll come early if that's OK ... about nine?"

She smiled. "Any time. See you Saturday."

He watched as she roared off down the street. At the junction, she hooted the horn then sped off back towards town. His mind was in a whirl. She had a way of looking at him that made him feel as if she thought he was really special. Yet he knew that couldn't possibly be true. She had made it clear that as far as Cindy Raven was concerned, the only really special guy in the world was hunky Carl Hickson.

3

Drew arrived at Cindy's just before nine on Saturday morning.

He switched off the engine and sat astride his bike for a minute or two gazing at the house. Although he'd heard of Manorfields, he'd never actually seen the houses there before. There were only four, each set well back from the road and surrounded by a huge garden. Cindy's was square, red brick with bay windows. "Mock Georgian," he supposed you called it.

Red roses grew over the front porch, and the garden was a palette of colour. Round the back he could just see the corner of a huge conservatory. In the garage were two cars, a sleek white sports car and a black BMW. Cindy's Mini was parked in the drive.

Drew took off his helmet and climbed off the bike. He took his tool kit from the box on the back and put his helmet in its place. He took off his leather jacket and slung it over the bike saddle.

He had been thinking about coming here ever since he'd fixed it with Cindy. Now, for some strange reason, he felt really nervous.

He stood in front of the double oak gates looking at the upstairs windows. In one bedroom, the curtains were still drawn. He wondered if it was Cindy's room. If perhaps she had forgotten he was coming and was still in bed.

He took a deep breath and opened the gate. As he did so, the front door opened and Cindy came out. She said something to someone inside then closed the door softly behind her. She was wearing scruffy track suit bottoms and a grey T-shirt. Her hair was scraped back into a pony-tail. She wasn't wearing any make-up and her eyes were red, as if she hadn't had much sleep.

She ran down the drive to meet him.

"Hi," said Drew, making a mock salute. "Your friendly mechanic's here to try and perform miracles with your limmo, Madam."

She smiled, although her eyes didn't light up in the way he had seen them light up before. She handed him the keys to her car. "I'm really grateful," she said.

Drew noticed she hadn't met his eyes. As she turned away he put his hand on her arm. Her skin felt smooth, cool beneath his fingers. He caught a hint of perfume. The same one he had smelt before. The one that reminded him of summer. "Cindy…? Is anything wrong … you look…?"

She turned to face him. To his horror, her eyes filled with tears. He saw her swallow. She didn't look up at him but began to fiddle with one of her fingernails. "My mum's really ill," she said, her mouth trembling. "The doctor came this morning … she's got to go into hospital."

"I'm really sorry … what's wrong with her?" Drew asked gently.

"Well … she's been sick ever since we came back from Oz. But not this bad. It's something to do with her kidneys. The doctor said she's possibly going to need a transplant."

"I'm sorry," Drew didn't know what else to say. "Look … do you want me to come back another time?"

Cindy brushed her hand across her eyes impatiently. She looked up at him with a wan smile. "No … it's OK, really. I'd be grateful if you *could* get it going. If Mum's going to hospital I'm going to need the car more than ever."

Drew put his tool kit down beside the car. "I'll see what I can do."

"Do you want me to stay and help?" asked Cindy.

"No, I'll be fine. You go back in. I'll give you a knock when I've finished," replied Drew.

"Right."

He watched her go back indoors. Her head was bowed and she looked suddenly small and vulnerable. It was all Drew could do not to run after her and take her in his arms. She really looked as if she needed a shoulder to cry on.

At the door, she turned and gave him a small smile. She disappeared inside and closed the door softly behind her.

Drew took a deep breath. He felt really sorry for

her, but what could he do? Where was Carl for goodness sake? He should be here comforting her. After all, he was her boyfriend.

It only took Drew a few minutes to find the problem with the car. It needed a new set of plugs. He had thought this might be the trouble and had stopped off at the local motor dealer's and bought a set on the way here. He fixed the new plugs and gave the engine a going over. The Mini was pretty old but in good condition. He didn't think it would give Cindy any more trouble for a while, although a good service wouldn't go amiss.

He put his tools away and wiped his hands on a rag. Then he put on his jacket and went to ring the doorbell.

Cindy's sister, Emma, opened the door. She had blonde hair like Cindy, but it was cut short, close to her head. She was still wearing her pyjamas and had an American football jacket over the top of them. She screwed up her eyes at Drew when he asked to see Cindy.

"Hang on." She turned and shouted up the stairs. "Cin, that biker's at the door."

Drew couldn't help grinning to himself. Through the door he could see a long, carpeted hallway. There seemed to be flowers everywhere, as if the garden had somehow spilled over into the house. At the far end, a glass cabinet was full of what looked like antique vases.

Cindy's sister was staring at him. "Do you want to come in?"

Drew shook his head. "No, thanks. I just wanted a word with Cindy."

Just then, she came running down the stairs. She had changed into her blue denim mini-skirt and had washed her hair. It fell like spun silk around her shoulders.

"Do you want to come in and wash your hands?" she asked.

"No, it's OK, thanks." Drew handed her the keys. "All done."

Her face lit up. "Already? Drew, you're fantastic. What was wrong with it?"

He explained. "... and it needs a service some time. I could do that but you'd need to bring it over to my place."

"OK. Look, Drew, let me pay you," said Cindy.

"You're joking," he said. "It only took five minutes."

"Please..."

"I said it's OK," he insisted. "I told you, I often look at friends' cars. It's good experience for me anyway."

"What about the plugs ... they must have cost something?"

"A couple of quid," he said. "But it's OK, really."

"Well ... I'll buy you a burger sometime, OK?"

He grinned. "If you insist."

She walked with him down the drive. "Carl's parents are coming over in a minute. They want to see Mum before she goes to hospital," she said. "Our families are really good friends."

"Oh?" Drew didn't let on he already knew. He didn't want her to know he had been asking Max about her. "What about Carl, isn't he coming with them?"

She shook her head. "He's got cricket practice this morning. He's going to try to come over later."

"That's pretty selfish of him—" Drew blurted it out before he had time to think.

Cindy shrugged. "He's hoping to make the local team, so he's got to be there. You know he's really good at sport. It's very important to him."

"Yeah?" Drew said. "More important than being here with you?"

She looked at him. "That's not fair, Drew."

"Isn't it?" Drew said sharply. Then he bit his lip. It really wasn't any of his business *what* Carl Hickson did in his spare time. All he knew was that if *he* had a girl like Cindy, he'd want to be there to support her if she needed it. "No," he said quickly. "Sorry. It's none of my business anyway."

"No," she said, flashing her eyes at him. "It isn't."

They stood by the gate. "Anyway," Drew said, "I hope your mum will be OK."

"Yes," Cindy sighed. "Me too."

He resisted the urge to put his hand over hers. "If there's anything I can do…"

She looked up at him. One eyebrow creased in a slight frown. There was something in her eyes that made her look as if she was seeing him for the first time. "Thanks," she said softly.

"Look," he began, "I'm sorry about what I said about Carl … as I told you, we go back a long way. We've never really seen eye to eye."

"No," she said. "I gathered that. Maybe you'll tell me about it some time. You know, me and Carl virtually grew up together, then we went to

Oz and I didn't see him for years. When we got back … well, he'd just grown into about the best looking guy I'd ever seen… I'd really like to know what he was like in those years I was away."

"Yeah?" Drew said, managing a grin. "Well I could tell you a few things but maybe it's better I don't."

She laughed. "No, maybe you're right. It doesn't really matter anyway. It's now that counts." She glanced up. "I'd better go. Thanks again, Drew. I won't forget that burger." She closed the gate behind him, watched as he put on his helmet and then gunned the engine. She waved. "See you."

At the end of the road, Drew passed a yellow Rolls purring its way towards Cindy's house. Carl's father, John Hickson, was at the wheel. He was big and beefy like his son. He wore sunglasses even though the day was cloudy. His hair was smoothed back and darkened with gel and his muscles had turned to fat long ago. Mrs Hickson sat beside him.

Drew couldn't keep his mind off Cindy all afternoon. She was so friendly towards him, so natural. And she *still* looked at him as if she thought he was someone special. Could it really only be his imagination? After all, she was still crazy about Carl. He just didn't know *what* to think.

He always did the same jobs at the hotel on Saturday. Sweeping up in the car parks and round the front entrance. Tidying the flower-beds, emptying the bins. Sometimes he disliked the job so much he thought he'd go mad. It wouldn't have been quite so rotten if he didn't have to wear those stupid green overalls.

He was just finishing up and trying to decide whether to work out in the gym before meeting Skip at the shopping mall when he saw Carl's car pull up in the car park. Carl got out and took his sports bag from the back seat. Drew frowned. Why wasn't he with Cindy? She really needed him right now.

Carl must have seen him staring because he came over to speak to him. Drew's heart sank. The last thing he wanted was a conversation with Hickson, he just might say something he regretted.

"Devlin."

Drew knew he'd got to keep cool. None of it was any of his business. He tipped his cap to the back of his head and leaned on his broom.

"Carl," he said evenly.

"I've been talking to Cindy," Carl said.

"Really? Well, that's a surprise seeing as she's your girlfriend," Drew said.

Carl's eyes smouldered. "Don't get smart, Devlin."

Drew made a mock salute. "No, sir. Sorry, sir."

"She said you fixed her car."

"That's right."

"I hadn't realized you knew each other so well," Carl said, frowning. "Lending her books ... now doing her car. What's going on, Devlin?"

"What do you mean, what's going on?"

"I mean, how come you're so friendly with my girl?"

"It's a free country," Drew said. He couldn't

believe what he was hearing. Surely Carl couldn't be jealous of him? He almost grinned at the thought.

"Yeah … well," Carl said. "Just don't get any ideas, that's all…"

"Would I?" Drew said.

"Not if you've got any sense."

"How's her mum?" Drew asked.

Carl's eyes narrowed. "What's it to do with you?"

"Nothing really. I just wondered, that's all. Cindy seemed upset this morning. In need of a shoulder to cry on."

"Yeah, well, they're all at the hospital." Carl gave a shudder. "I can't stand those damn places."

"So you're here instead."

"Right." Carl glanced at his watch. "Don't want to stop you working, Dev. My father doesn't reckon on paying people for doing nothing." Drew didn't miss the barely veiled threat. "See you."

Carl walked away, swinging his sports bag by his side. Drew went on leaning on the broom. He watched Carl stride up the steps and push his way through the front doors of the hotel. Why couldn't Cindy see what type of guy Hickson was? He just hoped she wouldn't be too hurt when she found out. He sighed. Well, didn't they say love was blind? He shook his head and carried on sweeping up.

Drew finished work at four and went to meet Skip at the shopping mall. He told his friend about Cindy and Carl.

"…and she can't see what he's really like," Drew

said. "I reckon all she can see is the good looks and a great body."

"Maybe that's all she wants to see," Skip said. He looked at Drew shrewdly. "Anyway, it's not really anything to do with you."

Drew took the last swig of his Coke. They were sitting on one of the seats by the fountains. The mall was packed with Saturday shoppers. "Tell me about it," he said with a grin. Then he looked more serious. "The thing is she's really nice ... I mean she's not *just* the greatest looking girl that ever walked on two legs ... she's got a really good personality to go with it. Sensitive ... you know." Drew leaned forward, his elbows on his knees, and stared at the floor.

"You're an expert, are you? Come off it, Drew, you've only spoken to her a couple of times," said Skip.

"I know." Drew crushed his Coke can and chucked it into the bin. "That's the trouble."

"Well, if I were you," Skip advised, "I'd forget her. Carl Hickson is the last person you'd want to mess with. Not if you want to keep your job, anyway."

"OK, OK, don't rub it in." Drew sat up. "Fancy going to the pictures tonight?" He knew he'd got to do *something* to get Cindy off his mind.

"What's on?"

"That new sci-fi film," said Drew.

"Great. Of course," Skip joked. "Bet you'd rather be going there with Cindy!"

"Yeah," Drew grinned. "But as you said the other day, beggars can't be choosers." He sounded light-hearted, but deep down he knew what Skip had said was true. Who was he kidding? It was obvious Cindy liked him as a friend but certainly nothing more.

Skip glanced at the clock. "I'd better get back, Marie's lost her key so if she gets home before me, she can't get in. Will you pick me up later?"

"Sure." Drew got up too. "Do you want a lift home now?"

Skip shook his head. "It's OK, I've got my bike." He raised his hand. "See you later."

Drew wandered down the mall, looking in the shop windows. He was just passing the florists, wishing he could afford to buy his mum a bunch of roses when he heard a familiar voice.

"Hi, Drew."

When he turned, Cindy was standing behind him. He wasn't prepared for the sudden lurch of his heart when he saw her.

"Cindy!" He tried to sound casual and normal. "Fancy seeing you."

She indicated the carrier bag over her arm. "I've just come to get Mum a few things."

"Is she OK?"

"Well, we've settled her in. She's got to go on one of those dialysis machines ... you know, they fix you up to it and it cleans your blood."

"Sounds terrible."

Cindy shrugged. "It's not too bad, it's better than dying."

She looked so unhappy Drew didn't know how he stopped himself from putting his arm around her. He had a fleeting vision of what it would be like to hold her in his arms. To feel her head resting against his shoulder, the soft silk of her hair against his face. He swallowed hastily and sought desperately for something to say. "My mum works at the hospital," he blurted out. "I wonder if she's on her ward."

Cindy raised her eyebrows. "Is she a nurse?"

"Yep."

"They're brilliant those nurses," Cindy said. "They were so kind..." She broke off and her eyes filled with tears. She brushed her hand across her eyes. "I'm sorry, I'm being a real wimp."

Drew put his hand on her arm. "No, you're not. Hey, come and have a Coke or something."

"We could have that burger if you like," she suggested, brightening up. "I'm starving, I haven't had anything to eat all day."

"Right, come on."

McDonald's was packed. They managed to find a seat over by the children's area. You could hardly hear yourself think.

Cindy put down her tray and dumped her carrier on the table. Drew sat next to her, his arm up against hers. She broke the seal on her milk shake carton and sucked some up through the straw. "Umm," she said. "Yummy."

When they had finished eating, she sat back with a sigh. "That feels better, I'm really glad I met you, Drew."

"I'm really glad you paid the bill," he said, grinning. "I'm broke as usual."

"Is that why you work at the hotel?" she asked. "It seems such a rotten job."

"It's OK," he fibbed. "And, yes, that is why I work there. I really need the money."

"Don't you get an allowance?"

He laughed. "An allowance, you've got to be joking." As soon as he'd said that he regretted it. Someone like her couldn't be expected to know what it was like to be really hard up.

She flushed. "Sorry."

"No, *I'm* sorry. You weren't to know. It's just that things have really been tough since—" He was going to say *since my dad went into prison* but stopped himself just in time. He really didn't think Cindy would want to know about his personal life. Anyway she had enough problems of her own to deal with.

But she was looking at him as if she wanted him to go on.

"Since what?" she asked.

He shrugged. "Nothing."

She was still gazing at him. "Look," she said. "I've been going on about *my* problems, why don't you tell me some of yours?"

"Didn't Carl tell you anything about me?" Drew had the sudden feeling that maybe Carl had taken pleasure in telling Cindy about his father.

"No," she said. "He just—" She broke off.

"What?"

"He just said he warned you not to get any ideas about me. He's pretty jealous of me talking to other guys ... I hadn't realized."

"I can't think why," Drew said lightly. "I'm hardly in his league."

She gave him a quick glance but didn't comment.

"You were going to tell me about your problems," she reminded him.

"Are you sure you really want to know?"

"Of course," she said. "What are friends for?"

And so Drew found himself telling her about his father. It was strange, his usual shyness around girls seemed to disappear. Maybe it was because she really looked as if she was interested in what he was saying. Most of the girls he knew only seemed to care about the latest fashions, or what was top of the charts that week.

He told her how tough it had been for them since his dad went away. She didn't look shocked or horrified as he thought she might. All she did was watch his face as he spoke to her, making noises of sympathy in her throat, now and then.

When he broke off, afraid he was rattling on too much, she shook her head. "I'm really sorry."

"Yeah, well..." Drew said. He finished his milk shake, noisily sucking the very last drop into his straw. He clasped his hands together on the table in front of him and stared at them. "So am I. You know..." He hesitated. He realized he was just about to tell Cindy something he'd never told anyone before.

"What?" she asked gently.

"I ... I sometimes feel it was all my fault, that's all."

Cindy gazed at him, her eyes glistening. "How on earth could it have been your fault?"

Drew shrugged and ran his hand through his hair. He leaned right forward, his elbows on the table. He steepled his fingers together. "I don't know … I just felt if I'd left school and got a job instead of insisting on going to college then I could have helped him. None of us had any idea he was in such debt."

Cindy bent across the table and put her hand over his. "It wouldn't have made any difference, Drew. You might not have been able to get a job and anyway … you couldn't have earned enough to help him out."

Drew swallowed. He could feel Cindy's soft fingers rubbing the back of his hand. He looked down to see them moving gently over his knuckle-bones as if she was testing the roughness of his skin. Her head was bowed, so close to his face he could smell the fragrance of her shampoo. He knew it was crazy but suddenly he wanted to cry. She'd think him a right wally if he burst into tears like a five-year-old kid. Especially in the middle of McDonald's.

"Maybe if he could have talked to me more," he said huskily. "You know what it's like when you're young … you're so tied up with your own problems you don't think about anyone else's, especially your parents'."

Cindy took her hand away. "That's true," she said. "I never really thought much of my mum being ill at first. I just thought it was the move back to England … that she was exhausted. Then it turns out she's really sick. I felt guilty, too, but she says I've no need."

"No," Drew said. "I'm sure you haven't."

Cindy glanced up at the clock. "Drew, I'm sorry, I'd better get going. I've got a date this evening."

"Yeah, me too." Drew began to wonder if he'd have time to go home before picking up Skip.

"We're going to see that new sci-fi movie," Cindy said. "How about you?"

"What a coincidence," Drew grinned. "So are we."

"I said I wasn't really in the mood," she went on. "But Carl insisted. He's been busy mowing his dad's lawn this afternoon."

"Yeah?" Drew almost said he'd seen him going into the fitness centre but thought better of it. He knew Cindy would be hurt if she found out Hickson had been lying to her.

"His dad insists he helps around the place," she said, half smiling to herself. "Mind you, he hates doing stuff like that."

"I bet," Drew said. He was surprised though. It didn't look as if Carl had everything handed to him on a plate after all.

Cindy began piling their empty cartons on to a tray.

"Look, Cindy," Drew said quickly. "I'm sorry if I was going on about my dad. It's not something I usually do."

"It's OK. As I said, what else are friends for?"

By now they had thrown the empty cartons into the waste bin. They walked out of the restaurant and headed towards the multi-storey car park where Cindy had left her car. Drew's bike was parked outside the mall.

"I'll see you around," Cindy said. "Probably at college."

"Right," Drew said. "Thanks for the chat. Don't

forget to let me know if there's anything I can do while your mum's in hospital."

She smiled up at him. "Thanks, Drew." The lift doors opened and she stepped inside. "Bye." She pressed the button. The doors closed and she disappeared from sight.

Drew turned and headed for the outside car park. His brain was in a whirl. One thing was for sure, the more he talked to Cindy, the more he liked her. He could tell she liked him too, and if she wanted to be his friend then it was certainly all right with him.

But whether it would be all right with Carl ... that was a different thing altogether.

4

Drew was late picking Skip up for the pictures. His neighbour had nabbed him on the way out wanting advice about his dismantled lorry in the front garden. When he and Skip eventually got to the cinema, the queue was enormous.

About half a dozen couples in front of them stood Carl and Cindy. Carl's powerful shoulders were hunched against the wind, his chin buried in his collar. Cindy had her arm linked through his, although they didn't seem to be saying much to each other. Cindy was staring at the movie poster on the wall while Carl was watching the traffic go past.

Inside, Drew waited while Skip went to get some popcorn. Carl was by the counter, holding the biggest carton money could buy. He seemed to be having an argument with the cashier.

Cindy waited by the ticket booth. She caught sight of Drew and came over, a smile on her face. She looked better than she had that afternoon.

She had piled her hair on top of her head and wore a pair of dark denims with a black leather jacket.

"Are you haunting me or something?" she asked Drew.

Drew grinned. "I reckon it's the other way round." Their eyes locked for a moment, then she lowered her gaze.

"Your date," she said. "She hasn't stood you up, has she?"

"She?" Drew suddenly realized Cindy had thought he was meeting a girlfriend. "No, I'm with Skip, you know, my mate from college."

"Oh," she looked confused. "I thought you…"

"No girlfriend, I'm afraid. Not at the moment anyway."

"Oh," she said again. "I'm surprised."

"Yeah?" Drew said. "Why's that?"

She shrugged. "I don't know really. I just assumed you would have that's all."

She was just about to say something else when Carl called loudly from over the other side of the foyer. "Cindy, you coming in or not?"

"Oops." She pulled a face at Drew and hurried away. Carl put his arm round her as she joined him, then together they went up the stairs to the circle.

Drew suddenly realized the last thing he wanted was to be seated near them. It wasn't only that he didn't want to be the target of any of Carl's comments. He didn't think he could bear to see them together … not close together, maybe even kissing. He was beginning to realize that his feelings for Cindy went far deeper than just friendship.

When Skip came back, he said. "Look, do you mind if we sit downstairs?"

"Why?" asked Skip.

Drew told him.

Skip shrugged. "OK, whatever you want. Mind you we've paid for—"

"I'll give you the difference," Drew said quickly.

Skip had to run to keep up with Drew as he headed for the doors. "It doesn't matter ... is anything wrong?"

The picture was just starting as they found some seats near the back.

"I said is anything wrong?" Skip hissed in Drew's ear over the thunderous opening credits of the movie.

Drew sat biting the inside of his thumbnail. "I told you," he said, "I just didn't want to sit near Hickson, that's all."

"Right." Skip glanced at him and he had the feeling his buddy knew there was more to it than that.

Skip sat back in his seat and began to stuff popcorn into his mouth. Drew did the same. It was a great movie, but to his annoyance, he couldn't stop thinking about Cindy and Carl all the way through. There was no doubt about it, he *had* to get her off his mind before he started to go crazy.

Drew was relieved that there was no sign of them when they came out. He had begun to think the less he saw of Cindy the better.

He was dismayed then, when he found her

waiting outside the Engineering block on Friday after lectures. Dismayed, yet pleased at the same time. She couldn't care *that* much about Carl's jealous streak. She held Drew's books in her hand. Drew tried to control the surge of pleasure he felt when he saw her standing there. He didn't succeed. He found his heart was beating like a drum when she smiled, the colour of her eyes highlighted by the deep blue of her T-shirt.

She waved the books at him. "I brought these back."

"So I see. Have you memorized them already?"

"No," she said, laughing. "I'm just so busy with my course and going to and fro from the hospital I think I'd better give up the idea for a while."

"You could have kept them," he said. "I told you there was no hurry for them back."

"Oh ... well, they're here now," said Cindy, almost apologetically.

"Thanks." He took them from her. "How is your mum, by the way?"

"She's getting on OK. She's going to come home soon and just go back to the hospital a couple of times a week to go on the machine."

"That's good then," replied Drew.

"Yes." Then she said, "Why didn't you tell me Carl was at the hotel the other afternoon when he'd told me he'd got to stay home and help his dad?"

"Umm." Drew racked his brains for an answer that wouldn't hurt her. He couldn't, so he decided to tell the truth. "Because I didn't want you to be upset," he admitted.

"Why should you care?" she said.

He shrugged. "I thought we were friends."

"Then we should tell each other the truth."

Drew shrugged his shoulders. "OK, Cindy. But look, it's really none of my business if Carl lies to you."

"No, but you could have said. I felt a real fool when I found out. Me telling you he was in one place when you knew he was somewhere else."

Drew couldn't help asking. "How *did* you find out?"

"I saw Max, he told me he'd seen you and Carl talking in the car park. Oh Drew, I hate being lied to."

"Yes," he said. "Me too. Cindy, I'm sorry."

Her face softened. She fiddled with the silver bracelet on her wrist. "Oh, it's not your fault. I'm still sore after our row that's all."

"Lovers' tiff?" Drew said lightly even though he felt like going to find Hickson and giving him a piece of his mind. Cindy had enough on her plate without this.

She smiled. "Oh, we made it up. He said he was sorry. It was just that he hates hospitals and didn't want to be roped in to visiting my mum."

"Yeah?" Drew said. "That's really selfish of him."

Cindy glanced up when she heard Drew's tone of voice.

"He can't help it."

"No," Drew said flatly.

"Anyway," Cindy began, "I'd better go. I've got to catch the bus. My dad brought me in this morning and Carl's got cricket practice again."

"What about the Mini? It hasn't conked out again?" asked Drew.

She grinned. "No. I forgot to get any petrol. Dad's bringing me some home in a can."

"I'll give you a lift if you like." Drew didn't know what had happened to his resolution to keep away from her.

Her eyes lit up. "Would you? I've always wanted to go on the back of a motorbike."

"What about Carl?" Drew said dubiously. "I don't want to cause any rows."

"Oh," her face fell. She screwed up her nose. "He can't really object, can he? You're only giving me a lift home."

"You should know," Drew said. "He's your boyfriend."

She hesitated, then suddenly seemed to make up her mind. "I'll just tell him the truth. It'll be OK."

"Right. It's up to you." Drew took the spare helmet from the bike box and helped her put it on. He swung his leg over the saddle and she climbed on behind him.

He looked over his shoulder. "You OK?"

"Yes, great." He could feel her arms, tight around his waist.

"Keep your feet tucked in," he said.

Her chin was resting on his shoulder. "OK."

He gunned the engine, put the bike into gear and roared off down the road. He felt her arms tighten as he accelerated towards the bridge.

He went the long way round. Through town, on to the bypass then along the river towards

Manorfields. All the way he was conscious of Cindy behind him ... her arms round his waist, her chest pressed against his back. Once, she shouted in his ear. "This is great. I love it."

"Good," he'd shouted back.

Then, about half a mile from home they passed Carl in his sports car, going in the opposite direction. Drew didn't know whether Cindy had seen him or not. But when eventually they pulled up outside her house and she clambered off, she said, "We passed Carl. Did you see?" She took off the helmet and bent her head to fluff out her hair. Her face was flushed, her eyes alive with excitement.

Drew sat astride the bike. He took off his helmet. "I don't know if he saw us. And even if he did, he may not have realized it was you with me."

She smiled suddenly. "I don't care anyway. That was so great it will be worth having a row for."

"Well, if you have any problems, let me know. I can soon square things with him."

"No, it's OK, I can fight my own battles, thanks," added Cindy.

Drew gazed at her. "Yes, sure."

She put the helmet into the box. "Do you want to come in for a Coke or something?"

"Er..." Her question took him by surprise. "I've got to go to work."

"Now?"

"Er ... well, not until later. I could come in for a minute if it's OK."

"'Course it's OK. My parents like me to bring friends home. Anyway, Dad's with Mum at the hospital and Emma's staying at Carl's. Aunty

Jane likes having her around." She grinned. "Good job someone does." She pulled his arm. "Come on, don't be shy."

"I'm not."

Drew switched off the engine and got off. He propped up the bike and followed her through the gate and down the path to the front door. She turned and smiled at him as she put her key in the lock. She opened the door and went in.

Drew stood on the threshold feeling unaccountably nervous.

"Come on, Drew," Cindy said impatiently. "Don't stand there like a lemon."

She led him down the hall. He had a vague impression of going past a luxurious-looking lounge with pine-clad walls and a huge, stone fireplace. One whole wall was filled with books.

The kitchen was huge. Almost as big as the whole ground floor of Drew's house put together. White units sparkled beneath an array of spotlights and the biggest electric cooker Drew had ever seen gleamed under a wide, copper hood.

Drew's jaw dropped. "What's this," he joked, "Buckingham Palace?"

Laughing, she made him sit down. She went to the fridge and took out two cans.

"Coke?" she said, turning.

"Great." Drew was still looking round in amazement. The only places he'd ever seen like this were in those glossy magazines you found in the dentist's waiting room. Even then, places like that didn't look real. More like a stage set put up just for the camera.

On one of the worktops was a thick photograph album. A few odd pictures lay scattered around. Drew picked one up. It was of Cindy and her sister taken on a sailing yacht. Cindy had her hair in long pigtails and looked about ten years old.

"This you?" he asked, although it was quite obvious that it was.

"Oh, no," she squealed and reached out to snatch it from him. "That's dreadful, you're not to look at it."

He grinned and held it out of her reach. "I already have." He stared at it, high above his head. "Quite a looker," he teased. "Even then." He still felt surprised at himself. Surprised how easy it was to talk to Cindy, to laugh with her. It just seemed like the most natural thing in the world.

She jumped and snatched the photograph from his fingers, almost knocking him over. He grabbed her arm and they wrestled, laughing. Her face was so close her could see the sparkles in her eyes and smell her perfume, light and flowery, the one he knew she always wore.

Suddenly she noticed him staring at her. Their gaze locked for a brief moment then she pulled away, her face becoming serious. She pressed her lips together. "Give it to me, Drew." The air between them seemed suddenly fraught with tension.

He handed it to her. "Sorry," he said.

She looked at it, then tucked it inside the album. "Don't keep saying sorry."

"Sorry," he said.

Their eyes met again and they burst out

laughing. The tense moment had passed as quickly as it had come.

She opened the album. "We've been making up a load of photos for Mum to look at in hospital," she said.

On the first page there were several snaps of Cindy and her sister on a huge yacht on a wide, azure sea. Cindy was wearing a bikini and had her hair tied up in a pony-tail. She was bronzed to a golden tan.

Drew looked over her shoulder. "How old were you then?" he asked.

She raised her eyes to the ceiling. "Twelve, I think," she said. "It was taken just outside Sydney." She turned the page. "Oh … this one's taken when we went to Florida," she laughed. "Look, there's Emma with Mickey Mouse…" She looked at Drew. "You ever been to Disneyland?"

Drew laughed. "Me? You've got to be joking. The last holiday we had was on the Isle of Wight and that was years ago."

"Well, I've never even *been* to the Isle of Wight," Cindy said, and they both laughed.

They thumbed through the rest of the album. "We lived in Sydney for four years," she said. "I didn't want to come back but Dad's project out there had finished."

There seemed to be pictures of Cindy and her family taken in all the exotic places of the world. A lot of earlier ones included Carl and his family. In each one Carl seemed like a miniature version of the boy he was now. Beefy, blond and in most instances, scowling.

Drew commented on the number of places they'd visited. "It looks as if you've been everywhere," he said.

"It's not really like that." Cindy explained. "It's just that Dad's always been so busy that holidays are really the only times we've been together as a family. That's why we made this up especially for Mum…" Her voice faltered and she put her head in her hands.

Drew touched her arm in sympathy. She took a deep breath then looked up at him, her eyes bright. "Sorry."

"Don't keep saying sorry," he said with a grin.

She smiled and showed him another page. On this one, Carl looked about ten years old. He was in a garden, wielding a cricket bat with an evil look on his face. Drew thought he looked just the kind of kid who would enjoy pulling the wings off butterflies, but he didn't say it.

Cindy gazed at the picture. "I use to hate Carl when I was little," she said. "He used to bully me like crazy. And Emma."

"I bet," Drew said.

"I couldn't believe he'd changed so much and grown into such a gorgeous hunk," she said. She looked at Drew. "Our parents are really pleased we're having a relationship." She smiled, a secret kind of smile that sent a pang of envy through Drew's heart. "I think they always hoped we'd … you know, get together."

"Yeah?" Drew didn't know what else to say.

"I know he's not the easiest of people to get on with," she added. "But when you really get to know him…"

Suddenly, Drew didn't want to hear any more. He just wanted to get away. Being so close to her had shaken him up more than he'd care to admit. He closed his eyes for a moment, trying to regain his balance. She'd die if she knew what kind of thoughts were going through his head. He took another swig of Coke and stood up.

"I've got to go," he said abruptly.

She looked surprised. "Aren't you going to finish your Coke?"

He took another swig and put the can down on the worktop. "Thanks. I'll see you, Cindy."

"Drew, wait." She ran down the hall after him. By the door she grabbed his arm. "Did I say something to upset you?"

He looked at her face, full of concern that she had done something wrong. "No," he said. "It's not you, it's me."

"What?" she frowned. "What's the matter?" She stamped her foot angrily. "Tell me, Drew. I thought we were friends."

He raised his hand and touched her lightly under the chin. The urge to take her in his arms and kiss her was almost overwhelming him. She was still gazing at him, a slight frown creasing her eyebrows. Then, as if she could read his mind, she gave a small gasp, a small intake of breath.

"Drew… I…" she began to say.

He heard her gasp again as he lowered his head towards her. He could see himself reflected in the moisture of her eyes. For one brief moment he thought she was going to let him kiss her. Then she seemed to come to. She put her hand firmly against his chest. "No, Drew."

He groaned and let his fingers drop. "Cindy, I'm really sorry."

Then he turned away from her. For one minute he could have sworn she had wanted him to kiss her. He never would have tried to otherwise. He opened the door and stepped out. When he tried to close it behind him he found she was holding the handle, standing there, watching him.

She was about to say something when the phone rang. She swore under her breath. "Drew … wait, please." She ran to answer it.

"Oh, hi, Carl. No, I got a lift home," Drew heard her say.

Drew was still on the doorstep. He closed his eyes and took a deep breath. He'd blown it now. He'd really blown it. He could have kicked himself. He had obviously misunderstood her. He should have known better. And if she told Carl what had happened, the guy would make his life hell. He wasn't scared of him … no way. But if he lost his hotel job it would be the last straw.

Cindy was still talking on the phone. "On the back of his bike," she was saying. "For goodness sake, Carl, it doesn't mean anything. Yes, of course I love you." Drew didn't wait to hear any more. He closed the door and strode down the path. He climbed on his bike, revved the engine and roared away. He screeched to a halt at the junction, then accelerated away down the road.

He didn't go straight home. He turned off at the roundabout and headed for the motorway. He hardly knew what he was doing or where he was going. All he knew was that he had to get the anger and jealousy out of his system. Anger at himself for messing things up with Cindy. Jealousy, if he admitted it, of the way he had heard her tell Carl she loved him. Speeding down the fast lane at seventy might just help.

The first vehicle he overtook was a pale yellow Rolls Royce. As he roared past he looked in his mirror. He recognized the figure of John Hickson at the wheel, smoking a big fat cigar. The cigar wasn't the only thing that was big about Carl's dad. He had a big stomach and a big, aggressive voice to match. He was always around the hotel throwing his weight about. He was entitled to, Drew supposed, seeing as he owned the place and about five other hotels as well. But somehow Drew couldn't imagine someone like Cindy having parents that were friends with a man like that. Not that it mattered. Nothing about Cindy mattered. Nothing about her was any concern of his.

He left the motorway at the next junction and took the road along the river. At the bridge, he parked the bike, climbed the stile and headed along the footpath. He turned off, pushing through the willows until he came to his favourite place. He took off his helmet and sat down on the bank. He picked a blade of grass, stuck it between his front teeth and stared moodily into the distance.

The late afternoon sun was warm on his back. He took off his jacket and lay down, his face up to the sky. He could feel the warm rays caressing his chest through the thin cotton of his T-shirt. Then, restlessly, he sat up again. He stared out over the water, his mind a whirl of conflicting emotions. A moorhen swam past with three chicks in her wake. Golden buttercups and a few vagrant blue-bells grew on the bank. Sitting there was like being in another world, a million miles from the noise and bustle of the town traffic.

He was still angry at himself. What a prize fool. Cindy must have seen how he was feeling. She must have seen the longing in his eyes. He had been kidding himself when he thought she felt the same. He remembered saying he would show her this place, now she'd never trust him enough to come with him. And if she told Carl... He didn't really want to think about it. One thing he was sure of, though, he had fallen in love ... *really* in love for the first time in his life. But that love had to be a secret ... for now ... probably for ever.

5

A week later, Max rang to ask Drew if he could look after the gym. "I've got to take my parents to the airport," he explained. "They're going back to Jamaica for a holiday. Would that be OK, Drew?"

"Sure," Drew said. "What time do you want me to be there? I've got some hours to put in around the hotel."

"I need to leave around five," Max said.

"That's fine, I'll ask Mr Appleby if I can knock off then."

"It's usually pretty quiet on a Saturday evening," Max said. "So there shouldn't be any problems. I'll pay you the going rate, of course."

But Drew wouldn't hear of it. He was glad to be able to repay Max's favours.

Drew spent most of Saturday cleaning up around the pool area and helping tidy the stock-room. He knocked off at four-thirty, showered and changed, then made his way through to the gym.

Max was waiting. "Here." He handed Drew a navy blue tracksuit with the Pavilion logo on the front. All the fitness centre staff wore them.

"Will you be back before I close up?" Drew asked.

Max shook his head. "No, just cash up as usual. If there's any problems you can get me on my mobile phone."

"There won't be," Drew said confidently. He'd been around the gym long enough to know the ropes.

When Max had gone, Drew changed into the track suit. He felt good in it. Better than those crummy green overalls. Maybe he'd ask Max if there was a job going in the gym permanently. It was about time he went up in the world. He combed his hair back with his fingers and gazed at himself in the full-length mirror. He was in pretty good shape. All those hours heaving weights were certainly paying off.

There were a dozen or so people using the exercise machines. Drew spoke to one or two of the people working out. No one seemed to need any advice, so he tidied up a few free weights that had been left out of the cabinet, then sat behind the counter reading one of Max's body-building magazines. He was just wondering if Cindy and Carl would turn up, when she came in on her own. After the evening he had given her a lift home, Drew wondered how she would react when she saw him. He need not have worried. Her face lit up when she saw him behind the counter.

"Hi!" She held his gaze briefly then looked down.

"Hi," he said softly. "How are you?"

She looked up again and smiled. She still looked tired. Her hair was pulled back in a pony-tail and she wasn't wearing a scrap of make-up. "OK, thanks," she said.

"How's your mum?"

"She's getting along all right."

"No word of a donor yet?" Drew asked.

Cindy shook her head sadly. "No. They say it could be tomorrow, or it could be months, there's just no telling. The strain's beginning to tell on my dad. He's going around like a bear with a sore head. That's why I came out. We've been at the hospital all day. I thought a work-out would do me good."

"It makes you wish you could do something to help."

"Yes," she said. "I wanted to have some tests to see if I could be a donor, but Mum won't hear of it."

Drew thought that was about the most unselfish thing he'd ever heard. "I guess she wouldn't want you to go through something like that," he said.

"Yes, that's what she said."

Cindy put her sports bag down and gave him her member's card to run through the ticket machine.

"Where's Carl?" Drew asked.

"Oh, he's gone out with his friends to that new club in town."

"Why didn't you go?" asked Drew.

"I just didn't feel like it. I said I was going to have a night in, then changed my mind."

"He won't like that," Drew said. "Especially if he knew I was here."

She sighed. "No. But I didn't know you would

be. And I can't stand those clubs, he knows that. I said I just wanted some peace and quiet and—"

Drew waited, but she didn't go on. "I'll turn the music down if you like," he said.

She smiled. "No, it's OK. I don't mind it here." She picked up her bag and went through into the changing room.

Drew watched her go. He wanted so much to take her in his arms, it was like a pain deep in the pit of his stomach. He felt so helpless. She was having such a bad time and there was nothing he could do about it. He wanted to tell her she was crazy, sticking with someone like Hickson. Couldn't she *see* how he was stringing her along? He was having a great time at the club, probably flirting as usual. But Drew knew she wouldn't thank him for telling her. OK, they were friends, but even friends didn't always want to hear the truth. Anyway, she loved Carl, for better or for worse, so it wouldn't make any difference what Drew said.

It was almost an hour later when the fire alarm went off.

It took Drew a couple of seconds to realize what was going on. The bell was tested every Friday evening and there were regular fire drills. Drew jumped off his stool. Today was Saturday. This was no test, this was "the real McCoy"!

Luckily, the gym was quiet now. Most people had finished their work-outs, showered and gone off to the bar for drinks. There was a man on the exercise bike and another using the dumb-bells. Cindy was nowhere to be seen. Drew had been so determined not to keep gazing at her he'd buried his head in a magazine and hadn't even noticed she'd finished.

Drew ran over to the man using the dumb-bells, shouting as he went. "Out! This is for real ... out as quick as you can!"

The man headed towards the changing room. Drew dashed after him and grabbed his arm. "You can't get your stuff, just get out, please. Wait in the staff car park so we know where you are!" The man ran out, followed by the guy who'd been using the exercise bike.

Drew knew the drill like the back of his hand. Even part-time workers like him had to know what to do in case of a fire. He dashed to the ladies changing room. He hammered on the door.

"Cindy!" he yelled.

There was no answer so he didn't hesitate. He pushed open the door and ran inside.

"Cindy!" he yelled again. He could hear the swish of the shower and a cloud of steam rose from the top of one of the cubicles.

"I'm in here," she called back.

"Cindy, you've got to get out!"

He grabbed a towel from the shelf and threw it over the top of the cubicle. She turned off the water and appeared with it wrapped around her. She blinked at him. "Isn't it a test?"

He pulled her arm. "For goodness sake, Cindy, no it isn't!"

She looked at him in horror. Water dripped into her eyes. "I can't go out like this," she pleaded.

"Yes, you can. Come on ... please," urged Drew.

He took her arm and they ran to the door, along the covered way and out into the car park. It was chilly out there. The sky was clear and a keen wind blew round the corner of the building with a sharpness like the edge of a knife.

People were spilling out of the fire exits. They were milling around, looking scared and confused. Drew left Cindy and ran over, ushering the people outside. He told them to stay where they were. Whether the fire was serious or not, they would need to know if anyone was missing. He helped an old lady who had stumbled coming out of the door. He took her bag from her hand and led her over to a group of people and left them all talking excitedly together.

Cindy was still standing where he had left her.

"I can't see any fire," she said. She began to shiver, hopping up and down to try and keep warm. "Drew, I'm freezing."

He took off his track-suit top and put it round her shoulders.

She looked up at him. "Thanks."

"Stay here, I'll go and see if I can find out what's going on," he said.

She held his arm. "Drew, don't go inside." There was something like panic in her voice.

"It'll be OK. It's probably a false alarm, but you can't be sure."

"Well, be careful." She was still shivering, hugging herself.

"I will," said Drew, seriously.

He met Mr Appleby coming out of the door. He told Drew what was going on. "It's just a small pan fire in the kitchen," he explained. "It set all the alarms off. We've got to wait until the fire brigade get here before we can go back in, though."

"Right." Drew ran back to where Cindy was still trying to keep warm. She was talking to one of the waitresses. He explained what had happened. The waitress went off to tell the others.

The fire engine turned up and screeched to a halt in front of the building. A couple of firemen jumped out and spoke to the manager, waiting by the gate. The firemen disappeared inside. A while later, the assistant manager came out, full of apologies, and began ushering people back inside.

"Come on." Drew put his arm across Cindy's shoulders and hugged her to him. "Before you get pneumonia."

She rubbed his arm, covered in goosebumps. "You're cold, too."

Then Drew heard someone call her name. John Hickson was hurrying across the car park. Instead of his usual business suit he wore baggy jeans and a polo shirt. He arrived out of breath.

Cindy turned in Drew's arm. "Uncle John!"

The manager hurried up to speak to him but Hickson waved him aside. "I'll be with you in a minute, George." He gazed at Cindy, then at Drew, still standing with his arm round her. "Cindy, are you all right?"

"Yes, I'm fine Uncle John, honestly."

"Thank goodness for that." He took a puff of his cigar then looked back at Drew. His eyes travelled up and down Drew's figure. "You work here, don't you?" he said, frowning.

"Yes, sir," Drew said.

"Uncle John, this is Drew Devlin," Cindy said. "He's been working in the gym this evening. He was great in getting us all out."

"Good, good. Remembered your fire drill, did you?" asked Mr Hickson.

"Yes, sir," Drew said.

"Well done." Mr Hickson patted Cindy absent-mindedly on the shoulder. "As long as you're all right, Cindy." The manager was still hovering behind them, wringing his hands together. The car park was almost clear now. "I'd better have a word with George," Hickson said.

Drew took his arm away from Cindy's shoulders as they went back through the door. She took off the track-suit top and handed it back to Drew. His fingers brushed hers as he took it from her. "Thanks," she said. "I'd better get changed."

By the time she came out, Drew had cashed up and was ready to take the money over to the reception desk where it was put in the safe over night. He was waiting to switch off the lights and lock up.

"Thanks for looking after me, Drew," she said.

He shrugged. "What are friends for?"

She stood close to him, her wet hair plastered back, her face flushed from the humidity of the shower room. A bead of moisture ran down her forehead. Without even thinking he raised his finger to wipe it away.

Drew never knew quite how it happened but suddenly his arms were round her. All he knew was that he wanted to kiss her more than anything else in the world. Nothing else mattered.

There was a thud as her bag fell to the floor. She was beating his chest. "Drew!"

But as he went to let her go, her arms went up round his neck and they were kissing. Softly at first, then more insistently. Her lips were soft and tasted like heaven. He heard her make a small noise in her throat. Her hands went up into his hair and she was pulling his head down as if she never wanted to let him go. He felt fire shoot through his veins. He began to tremble. He'd kissed a few girls before but nothing in the whole wide world had ever been like this.

Then, with a cry, she broke away. To his horror, tears were running down her cheeks. Before he could gather his reeling senses, she had grabbed her bag and flung herself out of the door.

"Cindy!" he shouted, but she had gone. Running across the car park as fast as she could. She wrenched open the car door and threw her bag in the back. Then she climbed into the driver's seat and fired the ignition. The Mini spun away, its tyres sending up a shower of gravel. It didn't stop at the entrance but with another screech of tyres she pulled straight out into the road and accelerated away down the street.

Drew watched until the red tail lights disappeared from sight. Then he sat down on the steps and put his hands over his face. He was still shaking. His knees felt like jelly. The kiss had been everything he had dreamed of. Every moment since he had first seen her standing by the college gates had been leading up to this.

What had possessed her he didn't know. But whatever it was he knew one thing for certain. She had wanted that kiss as much as he had.

He groaned and ran his hands through his hair. He felt stunned. Why on earth had she responded like that? Then he began to realize that, for Cindy, it had been nothing but one weak moment. She had been feeling fed up. Her mum was sick, her boyfriend had gone out without her, she had been scared by the fire. His chest rose in a deep sigh. Yes, that's all it had been. He wished that's all it had been for him, too.

Trying to pull himself together, he stood up, got the cashbox and locked up the gym. He was still feeling dazed as he deposited the box with the porter and said goodnight. He made his way out to the car park.

The wind had dropped and the sky was a vault of stars. Drew gazed up at them for a minute or two then got on his bike and rode home.

He couldn't sleep that night. He still felt dazed, confused. It was almost as if he could see the next few months unwinding in front of him like a slow reel of hopelessness. Bumping into Cindy at the gym, at college, seeing her with Carl. He knew it would tear him to pieces. But what could he do? Nothing, except get over it. He would have to put her to the back of his mind. It wouldn't be easy. In fact it would be the toughest thing he'd ever had to do in his life. But he knew, somehow or other, he had just got to do it.

Outside, Drew heard the sound of his neighbour's car pull up outside. In the distance a train rumbled its way towards the city. Then came the roar of a powerful motorbike on the main road. Drew turned over and eventually drifted off into a restless and uneasy sleep.

He was still in the same frame of mind by the middle of the following week. He hadn't seen Cindy or Carl since the night of the fire. He hadn't gone to the gym in case they were there. He couldn't face Cindy, not yet. And he certainly couldn't face Carl, especially if his father had told him he'd seen Drew and Cindy together. He could only hope Carl wasn't giving her a bad time over it.

He had avoided going into the college canteen in case she was there. Once he thought he had spotted her talking to a crowd of girls in the quadrangle, but it had turned out to be someone else entirely.

Then a few days later, he saw her.

He and Skip had been sitting on the grass with their shirts off, trying to get a suntan during the lunch hour.

"Hey, look," Skip had suddenly said. "There's the body beautiful."

Cindy was over by the gate, standing alone. She seemed to be looking for someone. She was wearing denim cut-offs and a blue shirt tied in a knot at the waist. Drew's heart turned over at the sight of her. He saw her glance at her watch. He wanted to rush over, to say "hi" and find out if she was OK. To find out if she would explain why she had kissed him as if she never wanted it to end. But he stayed where he was, watching her from afar and knowing it was the only thing he could ever do.

"So it is," he said, trying to sound casual but knowing he wasn't fooling his friend one little bit.

"Have you heard the rumours about Hickson?" Skip asked. He lay back, leaning on one elbow and chewing a piece of grass.

Drew looked at him sharply. "No ... what?"

"They say he's going out with a girl from Marie's school."

Drew stared at him. "What? Two-timing Cindy?"

Skip shrugged. "It's only a rumour ... someone saw them at that new club in town."

Drew felt a surge of anger. Trust Hickson! He'd always had a reputation for messing his girl-friends around. But Cindy! The guy must be crazy.

Skip was looking at him. "You going to tell her?"

"You're joking," Drew said. "It's nothing to do with me."

"No, that's true," Skip said.

Drew lay back on the grass with his face to the sun. He could hear the sound of a motor-mower from the playing field and the scent of newly cut grass drifted towards him on the breeze. He felt groggy, tired. He hadn't been sleeping well and for the first time since he started college, was beginning to find his course tough going. And now what Skip had just told him made him feel worse. He hated the thought of Cindy getting hurt.

The suddenly he heard her voice. "Hi, you two."

When he opened his eyes she was standing there, staring down at him. Drew felt his heart turn over.

He sat up quickly. "Hi," he said, annoyed to hear his voice come out in a squeak. He cleared his throat noisily.

He was suddenly acutely aware of the fact that this was the first time they had been near to one another since that crazy kiss. The kiss that he couldn't get out of his mind however hard he tried.

Cindy was gazing at him. She flushed slightly as their eyes met and he could tell by the expression on her face that she was remembering, too.

"How's your mum?" Skip asked.

Cindy looked surprised that he knew about her. She glanced at him. "She's getting on OK," she said.

"Is she still having dialysis?" Drew asked.

Cindy nodded. "She'll have to have that until she gets a transplant."

"Let's hope it's soon, then," Drew said. He didn't know what else to say. He couldn't imagine what it would be like to have to go through all that.

"Er, Skip," Cindy was saying. "Could I talk to Drew alone for a minute, please?"

"Er, yeah, sure." Skip scrambled to his feet. He gathered up his things. "See you."

"See you," she flung him a brief smile. "Can I sit down?" she asked Drew.

He spread his T-shirt out on the grass and patted it. "Sure."

She sat with her knees drawn up to her chin, not looking at him. "Drew, I really need to talk to you."

"Go ahead," he said. He tried to sound casual

although his heart was banging away like a drum in his chest, like a demented rock band.

She fiddled with the knot on her shirt as if she couldn't find the right words to say.

He leaned forward. "Cindy, if it's about the other night..."

When she looked at him, her eyes were bright with moisture. "Drew, I just can't stop thinking about it."

His heart leapt. Had he been right then? Had she really wanted that kiss as much as he had?

He took her hand. "Cindy..."

Just then the bell for afternoon lectures rang out. Drew let go and swore softly under his breath. He gathered up his books. "I'm sorry, I've got to go. I've got a really important lecture. I daren't miss it."

Looking crestfallen, she stood up. She picked up his T-shirt and handed it to him. He dragged it over his head.

Together, they hurried back across the grass.

"Drew, can I meet you afterwards?"

He groaned. He had arranged to go with Skip and a few friends to the pub by the river that evening. He'd promised Skip a lift and couldn't let him down. *And* he'd promised to look at someone's car after tea as well.

"I'm sorry, Cindy, I'm going out."

"No ... I meant straight after lectures."

"Cindy, I can't." He explained about the neighbour's broken down motor. "How about tomorrow lunch-time?"

"I'm playing squash ... and Friday. Er ... how about Saturday morning?" she asked.

He groaned again. "I'm sorry, I'm working."

She gave a small laugh. "Well, Sunday then?"

"Sunday ... OK. Where?"

Cindy looked thoughtful. "What about that place by the river ... the one you told me about?"

"Yes, sure," said Drew.

"OK," she said. "I'll meet you by the bridge. Would ten o'clock be all right?"

Drew hesitated. He was suddenly having second thoughts. Supposing Carl found out. "Cindy, I'm not really sure it's a very good idea."

She gazed at him. "It'll be all right, honestly. No one's likely to see us there, are they?"

"No ... OK," he agreed reluctantly. "No, I suppose not. Look, Cindy, I've really got to go."

He ran across to the Engineering block and through the door. He didn't look back, but for some strange reason, he had the uncanny feeling she was watching him until he disappeared from sight.

His mind was in a turmoil. She wanted to meet him, talk to him. Sunday just couldn't come round soon enough!

6

"I'm going to visit your dad tomorrow," Drew's mum said, when he got in from college. "Do you fancy coming?"

Drew hated going to the prison. He'd been several times but each time the ordeal got worse. He knew it was selfish but his dad didn't have much to say to him. They just sat opposite one another in silence half the time.

"Do you want me to?" asked Drew.

"Only if you want to, Drew. Sophie's coming so I won't be on my own," said Mrs Devlin.

Drew raised his eyebrows. His sister had only ever been to visit their father once. Perhaps, at last, she was coming to terms with what had happened.

"She's getting brave," he commented.

"Your dad especially asked to see her."

"Oh." Drew lifted his eyebrows. "Not me though?"

"He said you can please yourself." Drew's mother gave him a piercing look.

"Do you mind if I don't?" he said, feeling guilty.

"No. I know how you hate it."

Drew looked at his mum. "I'm really sorry."

"It's all right, Drew. I understand. Although it's an open prison it's still a terrible place. Maybe when your dad gets home you'll feel differently about what happened."

"Yeah," Drew said, not at all convinced and still feeling guilty. "Hope so."

He was still thinking about his father as he rode to pick up Skip. He knew his mother was hoping his dad would get parole and be home soon. She talked about it all the time. It would seem really strange having his father around the place again, just when he'd got used to him not being there. Maybe, in time, they could get back to being a normal family again.

Skip's sister, Marie, was standing by the front gate when he arrived. She had borrowed Skip's leather jacket and wore it over white jeans and a skimpy striped top. She had on gold earrings and wore bright pink lipstick. Her hair was long and loose, caught up on one side with a gold clip.

She gave Drew a big smile as he pulled up by the kerb.

He switched off the engine and took off his helmet. He grinned at her. Skip was right. Marie certainly did look a lot different when she was dressed up.

"Hi, Drew. Is it OK if I come with you? Skip had to go and see someone about a holiday job. He said he'd meet us there."

"Sure," Drew said. He gave her a sideways look. "You sure your mum knows you go in pubs?"

She laughed. "Come off it, Drew. I'm not a kid any more."

"No," he said, looking her up and down. "I can see that. He leaned forward. "What's happened to the specs?"

She blinked her long eyelashes at him. "Ever heard of contact lenses?"

"Umm," he said, grinning. "You look a lot better without them. Shame about the freckles though."

She gazed up at him, laughing, then punched his arm. "Thanks a bunch. Are we going or are we going to stay here so you can insult me?"

"I was only kidding," he said and realized he meant it. The days when Marie was a scrawny kid were long gone.

"I know," she said, still smiling up at him. "Anyway, I'm used to it. You and my brother are as horrible as one another."

Drew turned and took the spare helmet from the bike box. "Stick that on."

Marie buckled it on and climbed on behind him. She put her arms round his waist.

"OK?" he asked.

"Great."

When they arrived, Skip was nowhere to be seen. There were a couple of their friends sitting in the garden. They waved as Drew and Marie took off their helmets.

"Over here," one of Marie's friends called.

The pub was a quaint, "olde worlde" place set on the banks of the river. The garden was dotted with tables and chairs, and wooden benches had been set out along the edge of the water.

"You go on," Drew said. "I'll get the drinks. What would you like?"

"Oh, er, Diet Coke, please," Marie said, heading off. Half-way, she turned. "And a packet of crisps."

"Right," said Drew.

The bar was crowded and by the time Drew got back with the drinks, Skip had turned up. Marie was busy chatting to her friend, Donna. They were discussing the merits of the latest song that was top of the charts.

"Sorry you got lumbered with Marie," Skip said. "Dad dropped me off on his way to a meeting."

Drew put the drinks down on the table. "No problem," he said. He sat down and put Marie's drink on the table in front of her.

"Thanks." She beamed him a smile. Donna said something to her and they both giggled.

"Any luck with the job?" Drew asked Skip.

"Yeah. A friend of Dad's wants me to work on his building site during the summer. Great, huh? Not quite like your cushy number at the hotel," Skip said with a grin. "But better than nothing."

"Cushy number…" Drew began indignantly. Then a couple more friends arrived. Skip got up to go with one of them to the bar. Drew took a mouthful of his Coke and stared out over the water. The voices of his friends seemed to recede into the distance. He felt detached, somehow not part of their world. He stared into the water as if it had hypnotized him. It drifted past sluggishly. If it wasn't for the occasional bit of wood or clump of water weed floating past you would hardly know it was moving at all. Somehow his mind kept slipping back to Cindy. He didn't know if it had been his imagination but she had looked really disappointed when he said he couldn't meet her after college. He wondered again what it was she wanted to speak to him about. She had said she couldn't stop thinking about that kiss. Well, neither could he. And where did Carl fit into all this? She must still be going out with him or she would have said. He felt so confused it was driving him crazy.

"Drew!" He suddenly realized Marie was nudging him.

"Oh." He came to. "Sorry, what did you say?"

She didn't seem to mind he'd been miles away. She repeated what she'd said.

"I said Donna would like a ride on your bike some time."

"Oh," he said absent-mindedly. "OK."

It was a lovely evening. Balmy, with a slight breeze that kissed the branches of the weeping willows and made them tremble. The pub garden was beginning to fill up. Drew recognized one or two other people from college.

"This is a really nice place." Marie looked round as she took another mouthful of her drink. She leaned back and stretched out her legs.

"Yes." Drew sat up. He was beginning to think this evening was going to be a disaster. It wasn't anyone's fault. He just wasn't with it. He should have agreed to meet Cindy and found out what she wanted to say. Then maybe he wouldn't be thinking about it all the time. Skip had got here without him anyway so he wouldn't have been letting him down.

He glanced at Marie. She was tapping her toe to the rhythm of the rock music that had started emanating from the door of the public bar. Then she began to sing softly. It was the song that was top of the charts and she knew all the words.

"I'm getting this for my birthday," she said in between verses. "Mum's promised me the tape."

"Something else will be top by then," Drew said.

She giggled. "Yes, probably. I'll still like this one, though. They're a fabulous band. Really hunky." She went on humming and tapping her feet.

"You want to wait until it's on a compilation album. You'd get all the top ones, then," added Drew.

"You're as bad as Skip." She punched his arm playfully. "Telling me what to do."

Drew grinned at her but his heart wasn't in it. He suddenly felt he had to get away. He mumbled something about going to the loo and made his way up the garden towards the saloon bar. Inside it was crowded and noisy. He said "hi" to one or two people he knew then threaded his way to the gents. Inside, he leaned his head against the wall for a minute and took a deep breath. This wasn't going to be one of the most brilliant evenings of his life, that was for sure.

The door opened and someone else came in. He glanced their way. Then he froze. Carl Hickson stood there looking as surprised as Drew. He looked him up and down, obviously taking in his leather jacket, jeans and white T-shirt. Carl was wearing a pale crushed linen suit with a collar-less shirt and expensive-looking brown leather shoes. As usual, he looked like something from a fashion ad.

Drew felt like sinking into the ground. Of all the people. He could have kicked himself. He knew this place was popular with the college kids but he hadn't thought Hickson might be here.

"Devlin," Carl said with his usual derisive grin. "Fancy seeing you."

"Yeah," Drew said coolly. "Fancy seeing *you*." He headed for the door. The last thing he wanted was to get into conversation. By the expression on Carl's face it could only lead to trouble.

Hickson barred his way. "Actually," he said, "I'm glad you're here. I wanted a word." He spoke evenly but Drew recognized the underlying aggression in his tone.

"Yeah?" Drew tried to sound relaxed. "What about?"

"Cindy," Carl said bluntly.

"Cindy?" Drew clenched his jaw tightly. He could feel a small muscle moving in his cheek. If Carl started on about Cindy he didn't know how he was going to control his temper. He felt on edge as it was. All it would take would be one wrong word for him to land Carl that punch he'd been promising himself for ages. He looked at Carl from under his dark brows. "What about her?"

"My dad was telling me he saw you with her the night of the fire at the hotel," Carl said. He fiddled with one of the buttons on his jacket.

"So?" Drew folded his arms and leaned against

the basin. "I was working in the gym. It was my job to get her out. And everyone else, as it happened," he added although he didn't really know why. He had no need to justify his actions to anyone, let alone Carl.

"He said you two seemed like old friends," Carl said.

"Yeah?" Drew looked Carl in the eyes. He noticed how pale they were, pale and cold. He knew his attitude was making Carl worse but he couldn't do anything about it. The guy got right up his nose and that was that. He might be able to bully a lot of people but Drew Devlin wasn't one of them. He should know that by now.

Carl was breathing heavily. Beads of sweat were breaking out on his brow. He was really getting stewed up about something. Then Drew felt a sudden stab of alarm. Supposing Cindy had told him what happened *after* the fire? He almost groaned aloud. If she had, it looked as if he could kiss his job goodbye. He needed a load of new books for college and his bike needed a new tyre. There was no way he could go without his wages. It looked as if he'd blown it again.

"I've already warned Cindy about you," Carl was saying.

"Yeah?" He *had* to keep cool. For Cindy's sake, for his own, for his mum who needed his contribution to the housekeeping. He couldn't let Carl see he wanted more than anything to punch his face in. He remembered the good feeling he'd had when he'd done it before. It had been worth having sore knuckles for a week.

"Are you listening, Devlin?" Carl narrowed his eyes.

"Yeah, yeah," Drew said. "You've warned Cindy about me. Well thanks, Carl. I'm sure she was grateful."

He went to push past. As he did so, Carl shot out his hand and grabbed the front of Drew's jacket.

"Lay off!" Drew said angrily. He tried to push him away.

Carl pulled his face close. "If I hear your name linked with Cindy's again, Devlin, you'll be out of that job faster than you can blink."

Drew's patience ran out. Suddenly he didn't care about his job, or Cindy, or his mum. All he cared about was Carl Hickson. He put both his hands on Carl's broad shoulders and gave him a really hard shove. Carl staggered backwards. Drew had tried, he'd really tried to keep his temper. He caught sight of himself in the mirror. Nostrils flaring, eyes blazing. Almost, but not quite as tall as Carl, almost as broad. He strode towards him. "And supposing I tell Cindy there's a rumour you're seeing a girl from the High School at the same time as going out with her? What then, Hickson?"

Carl's jaw dropped. He lunged forward but Drew was too quick for him. He dodged to one side. Carl shot past, colliding heavily with the hand drier on the wall. He turned swiftly and lunged again. For a minute, the two boys wrestled, then, suddenly, the door opened and Drew felt himself being hauled away.

The barman pinned back Drew's arms. "What the hell's going on here?"

Drew wrenched away from his grasp. He straightened his jacket. Carl was panting, glaring at Drew as if he could kill him.

"Nothing," Drew said. "Right, Carl?"

Carl's face was scarlet, furious. "Right," he muttered.

"OK, well just cool it, you two. If you've got differences to settle, do it somewhere else, OK?"

"Right," Drew said.

The barman looked from one to the other then went back outside.

Drew went to the sink and turned on the tap. He filled his cupped hands with water. To his annoyance he found he could hardly control their shaking. He rinsed his face. Somehow he knew that Carl wouldn't go for him again. Carl had produced a comb from his pocket and was carefully combing his hair back into place. Drew noticed *his* hand was shaking, too. It made him feel a whole lot better.

Carl looked at Drew in the mirror. "If you say anything to Cindy," he said quietly, "I swear you'll not only get the push from the hotel, I'll make sure you never get another job in this town. My dad knows everyone. It would only take one word."

Drew breathed deeply. Suddenly he couldn't be bothered any more. He felt sick and depressed, as if he'd gone through a storm and come out the other side the worse for wear. Being friends with Cindy Raven had brought him nothing but grief.

As far as he was concerned, Carl was welcome to her.

"Get lost," he muttered. He headed for the door, went through and slammed it shut without looking back.

Outside, Marie was sitting on her own. The others had gone for a walk along the river path and Skip and another guy were having a game of darts in the public bar.

"Drew, where've you been?"

He sat down and put his arm across the back of the seat. He rubbed his hand round his jaw. "I met someone I knew."

She was frowning at him. "Are you OK? Your hair's all messed up." She put up her hand and patted it down. Drew looked at her. She was staring at him, her face was full of concern. "Are you sure you're all right?" she said, still puzzled.

"Yes, honestly." He put his hand on her shoulder and gave it a gentle squeeze. He managed a grin. "Don't look so worried."

There was a fly drowning in his Coke. He fished it out then threw the drink on the grass.

"Fancy another?" he said to Marie.

She had torn her eyes away from him and was looking over to where someone stood under the willow tree, staring at them.

"Er, yes, please. Hey, that girl looks as if she knows you," she said.

And when Drew glanced over he saw it was Cindy. She had an expression on her face that he had never seen before. Surprise? Dismay? He really didn't know. All he knew was that as their eyes met he could only manage the briefest of nods before Marie had stood up and was pulling at his hand.

"Come on," she said. "I'll come with you to the bar."

He allowed himself to be dragged up out of his seat.

When he looked back to the place where Cindy had been standing, she had gone.

He ended up giving Marie a lift home. Skip had gone on ahead in someone's car. The others had drifted off in dribs and drabs. Altogether, Drew thought it was the lousiest evening he'd ever had. After the encounter with Carl, then seeing Cindy, he had hardly been able to bring himself to talk to anyone. He knew he was being rotten company but somehow he couldn't shake off his mood.

At her gate, Marie handed him the helmet. "Want to come in?"

He shook his head. "No, thanks. I'll toddle on home."

Marie was looking at him shrewdly. "You seem really cheesed off, Drew," she said.

"Yeah. Well, I'm sorry if I spoiled your evening."

She shrugged. "You didn't. But if ever you want to talk…"

Drew managed a grin. It seemed crazy, Skip's little sister wanting to act as counsellor. Only she wasn't his *little* sister any more. She had grown into a young woman. A pretty attractive one at that. Maybe that's what he needed to get over Cindy? To take someone else out. Someone who was free and didn't have a jealous boyfriend whose hobby was bullying people. He liked Marie a lot. Like her brother she had a good sense of humour. She might be just the tonic he needed.

"Thanks, Marie," he said. "Look, I'm just going through a bit of a bad time at the moment, that's all. I'll get over it, don't worry." He sounded more optimistic than he felt.

"I hope so." Marie turned to go.

He put his hand on her arm. "Hey, maybe we could go out some time … just you and me?"

She smiled. "You'd have to cheer up a bit," she said.

"I'll try, I promise."

"OK," she said. "That would be great. Hey, are you going to the college disco on Friday?"

Drew hadn't given it a thought. He vaguely remembered seeing a poster on the notice-board. "Er … yes, possibly," he said.

"I might see you there, then," Marie said.

"Yeah," he said. "OK."

He watched her walk up the path. Before she opened the front door she turned and waved. "See you," she called.

He stood there for a minute, staring at the closed door. Then he gunned the engine and headed home feeling more lonely and miserable than he had ever done in his life.

7

"So, your dad will be out soon?" Skip said.

"Uh-huh." Drew sucked his Coke through a straw. It was Friday evening and the two boys were having a burger directly after college. "He told mum when she went to visit him. If his parole goes through he'll be home the middle of next month."

"She must be pleased," said Skip.

"Yes, she is." Drew remembered she had come back from the prison with a great big smile on her face. Drew had got mixed feelings. He was glad his dad was being released early but felt full of anxiety at the thought of having him around the house again. It would take some adjusting to, that was for sure.

"You don't look as if you're very pleased," Skip said.

Drew shrugged. "It'll just seem strange, that's all. I mean he's been gone almost two years." He glanced at the clock. "Better get going," he said.

"I've got to put in a couple of hours around the hotel before the disco." He had decided to go after all. It was no good moping around like a wet blanket. He had to get out and at least try to enjoy himself.

"You haven't given up heaving those weights around, have you?" Skip asked after they had paid the bill and were on the way to the car park.

Drew shook his head. "No, but I'm thinking of trying to find somewhere else. Trouble is Max lets me train for free."

"Why leave then?" asked Skip.

"Because I keep seeing Cindy there and it only causes hassle." He had already told Skip about the encounter with Carl.

They walked down the stairs. "You don't have to talk to her," Skip pointed out.

"No, I know," agreed Drew.

"What about Sunday?" Skip asked. "Aren't you supposed to be meeting her?"

"Supposed to be," Drew said. "But I don't think I'm going to turn up."

Skip looked as if he didn't believe him. "Yeah, I bet. You won't be able to resist."

Drew swallowed. Ever since the other night he had really made up his mind he would do everything to avoid seeing Cindy. It had been hard to refuse when she said she wanted to meet him. But, when he thought about it, it was a stupid idea. He had been influenced as usual by those blue eyes and the way she looked at him as if he was the only person in the universe. OK, so she might still be thinking about that kiss. But maybe she was *regretting* it. Maybe *that's* what she wanted to talk about. After all, she was still going out with Carl, wasn't she? So it couldn't have meant *that* much to her.

Skip was regarding him shrewdly. "Well, I reckon you'd be doing the right thing."

"What? Not turning up?"

"Uh-huh. Look, Drew, Cindy's really turning out to be bad news. She's stringing you along. One minute she says she's crazy about Hickson. Then she kisses you like there's no tomorrow. Next minute she's asking to meet you. What's she up to?"

Drew shrugged. "No idea."

"Have you ever thought that maybe she really wants Hickson to know?"

Drew frowned. "What are you on about?"

"Don't you think it's just possible she's found out he might be two-timing her?"

"How?"

"Well, you know how rumours get around. She's bound to hear about it sooner or later."

"So what's that got to do with meeting me?" asked Drew.

Skip shrugged. "Maybe she wants to pump you for information? She's seen you with Marie. Perhaps she's found out the other girl goes to the same school. She might even want to make Carl jealous."

"Skip, she isn't like that. Anyway, your imagination's running away with you as usual. She just want to talk about something."

"Maybe *that's* what she wants to talk about.

Anyway, how do you know she isn't like that?" asked Skip.

"I just know, that's all," said Drew.

Skip sighed. "Well, it's up to you. But if you ask me, *not* turning up to meet her would be the most sensible thing you've done in years."

"Who's side are you on?" Drew asked.

"Yours." Skip looked at him. "Look, old mate. There's nothing I'd like better than to see you get the girl of your dreams. But I just don't reckon she thinks of you in that way."

"Yeah, well you're probably right. It would be crazy to go and meet her. As far as I'm concerned the less I see of her, the better," said Drew.

And he meant it.

Later, when he'd thought about it some more, he reckoned Skip could be right. What *was* Cindy up to? Perhaps she *was* stringing him along. Since that night in the gym she *must* know how he felt about her. And her response to that kiss ... he *still* couldn't forget it. But maybe she had been faking. Just using him. Some girls were like that. Using one guy to make another jealous. But Cindy? He really couldn't believe she would do a thing like that. Maybe he had misjudged her. The more he thought about it, the more he decided it could be true.

The disco was in full swing by the time Drew arrived. He had been late leaving work and by the time he had showered and changed it was almost ten o'clock.

He put his jacket and helmet in the cloakroom

and headed for the hall. On the way he saw Carl Hickson standing by one of the corridor fire exits talking to someone. His heart sank. Carl and Cindy were the last people he wanted to see. He'd been stupid not to realize they'd be there. He almost turned and went back the way he had come. Then he took a deep breath. He'd be bound to bump into them again sooner or later. At the gym, at college. He *had* to face them some time. Now seemed as good a time as any.

When he got closer, however, he saw the girl wasn't Cindy at all. She was a shorter, blonde girl of about sixteen. More Marie's age than Cindy's. Carl was leaning with one elbow against the wall, looking down at her. Drew saw him touch a lock of her hair and say something in her ear. He felt a sudden flare of anger. Cindy could be visiting her mum in hospital while Carl was flirting around with another girl. If it was the girl from Marie's school it looked as if that gossip might be true. Didn't the guy ever think of anyone but himself?

Luckily, a crowd of people began pushing past Drew and he went along with them into the hall. Out of the corner of his eye he saw Carl and the girl part company. She went over to talk to a couple of friends and Carl headed off towards the main doors.

The place was packed. Not only were most of the people from Drew's year there, it seemed half the young people of the town had turned up.

As usual, the different college groups weren't mixing. All the guys and girls from the Technical blocks were on one side of the room, the students from the academic faculty on the other.

Drew stood on tiptoe and spotted Skip and a few of their friends propping up the bar. He pushed his way across the dance floor. The sooner he got out of the crush, the better. He nodded to one or two people he knew then arrived to slap Skip on the back.

"You made it." Skip gave him a broad grin.

"No, I'm just a cardboard cut out." Drew sounded a lot more cheerful than he felt.

"I'd almost given you up," said Skip.

"Sorry, I was late getting off work," said Drew.

Drew bought a Coke and stood watching the dancers. He recognized one or two girls he'd been at school with. Even an old flame, dancing with a guy in baggy trousers and a vest.

Then the music changed and the strobe lights stopped flashing. One single globe spun above the floor. It sent whirling, starry patterns across the faces and bodies of the dancers. A few wandered off to sit down, but most found a partner. Soon the floor was covered with couples swaying to the soft rhythm of the music.

Drew heard a voice at his shoulder.

"Hi, Drew."

He looked round to see Marie gazing at him. He felt again that flicker of surprise that Marie had turned into such a great looking girl.

"Want to dance?" she said.

"Er … yeah, sure." He put his can on the bar.

He took her hand and led her on to the floor. The song had changed again. Something smooth and slow, a tune Drew recognized but couldn't put a name to. He put his hands on Marie's slender waist. She lifted her arms up round his neck and smiled up at him.

"You feeling any better?" she asked.

"Yeah," he fibbed. "Better now I've seen you."

She looked as if she didn't believe him. "Yes, I bet."

"Honestly," he said, meaning it. Marie looked even more attractive than she had done when they went to the pub. She wore a tight-fitting black dress way above her knees. Her hair was long and loose. She smiled up at him then wriggled her shoulders and folded her body into his. Drew closed his eyes and swayed to the gentle rhythm of the song. He held Marie tightly. Her fingers moved softly, stroking the back of his neck between his hair-line and the collar of his shirt. Then she ran her hands down over his shoulders and down the muscles of his back. It felt good, made him relax. He was amazed at the amount of tension he was carrying. He could hear Marie humming along to the music. He buried his face in her soft hair. It smelt good, a hint of musk in her shampoo. He couldn't help it but he began to wonder what it might be like to dance with Cindy this way. To feel her pressed up against him. To feel the softness of her hair against his face…

He opened his eyes suddenly. He'd had an odd feeling someone was staring at him.

There was a couple next to them, squashed in so close the boy almost trod on Drew's foot.

Drew felt a stab of irritation when he realized

who it was. Carl and Cindy... And Cindy was staring at him over Carl's shoulder. So she *was* here after all. He wondered where she had been while Carl was with the other girl.

When their eyes met, she smiled quickly and mouthed "Hi" at him.

"Hi," he mouthed back. He hoped Marie wouldn't notice how fast his heart had begun to beat.

Cindy smiled again then quickly dropped her eyes. Carl turned to see who she had spoken to. She said something in his ear and steered him quickly away. He turned and glared at Drew. Drew ignored him and once again buried his face in Marie's hair.

Marie had been watching. "Who was that?"

"Oh ... no one. A friend from college, that's all. Her name's Cindy."

"She was the girl at the pub the other night," said Marie.

"Yeah, that's right." Drew tried to sound casual.

"Who's the hunky guy?"

"Her boyfriend, Carl Hickson."

"I've seen him hanging around the school gates," Marie said. "I thought he went out with someone in the sixth form but it's not *that* girl."

"Yeah, I'd heard," Drew said bitterly. "He's not exactly famous for being true to one person."

Marie leaned back and stared him in the face. "You sound as if you're jealous."

"Rubbish," Drew pulled her close again. "She's just a friend, that's all. I don't like seeing people being messed around."

"You're an old softie," Marie said with a giggle.

114

"That's me," he said, managing a grin.

He closed his eyes again and tried to concentrate on the music.

When the dance ended he took Marie back to the bar. He finished his drink and turned, leaning his elbows on the counter. In spite of himself, his eyes scanned the dance floor looking for Cindy and Carl. He just couldn't help it.

He caught sight of them at last. They were standing with a crowd of friends by the door. Then Cindy said something to Carl and disappeared outside.

Suddenly Drew knew he had to talk to her. He *had* to tell her he'd decided it would be a really stupid idea for them to meet on Sunday.

The music had started up again by now and the floor was crowded again. Carl was nowhere to be seen. Then Drew caught sight of him dancing with the girl he had seen him with earlier. Hopefully, he would be occupied for a while.

Drew pushed his way towards the door. He was still a few metres away from the entrance to the girl's cloakroom when he saw Cindy come out. Instead of going back inside she slipped out through the swing doors.

Drew ran out after her.

It was a calm, moonlit night. The dark sky was clear and dotted with a million twinkling stars.

She was sitting on the wall of the fountain in the middle of the flood-lit quadrangle. She was gazing into the water. Her hair was loose and wild. She wore tight black leggings, with Doc Marten boots, a white shirt with a short, studded black leather jacket. Her skin glowed in the lights from the lamps. Drew saw her lift her face to the breeze and close her eyes. He watched her for a moment, his heart thudding. She looked so beautiful he felt a lump come to his throat. Then, knowing time was short, he softly called her name.

"Cindy."

She turned swiftly at the sound of his voice. A quick smile lit up her face. Then she grew serious. She glanced over to the door then back at Drew. Closer now, he could see she had shadows of tiredness beneath her eyes.

"Drew you shouldn't be here... Carl might—"

"It's OK, he's dancing with someone."

She frowned suspiciously. "Oh? Who?"

"I don't know," Drew said quickly. If Cindy hadn't heard the rumours about Carl then he didn't want to be the one to tell her. "Some kid from the High School. Cindy ... look, I wanted to talk to you."

She got down from the wall and stood facing him. Her eyes were glittering with starlight. "I think we'd better leave it until Sunday, Drew."

"But..."

"Look, Drew," she interrupted. "Carl was hopping mad you gave me a lift on your bike. *And* his dad told him we were together the night of the fire so if he sees us here together—"

"Yes," he interrupted. "I know."

She frowned. "How do you know?"

He told her about his encounter with Carl at the pub.

116

She looked horrified. Her hand flew to her mouth and her eyes filled with moisture. "Oh, Drew. I'm really sorry."

He shrugged. "It was no big deal." He didn't want her to know how angry he had been. How determined he was never to have anything to do with her again. It would seem stupid, anyway. Here he was, not able to take his eyes off her … all his resolutions crumbled away into dust.

"You know, he *could* make things really tough for you at work if he wanted to," she was saying. "I really don't want that to happen. I've told him he's crazy, that we're just friends. He won't listen to me. He just says a load of rotten things about you."

Drew frowned. "What does he say about me?"

"Oh, you know … about your dad and stuff."

Drew's nostrils flared with anger. "Yeah, well he would, wouldn't he."

Cindy glanced at him then looked down, fiddling with one of the silver studs on her jacket. "That doesn't make any difference to me, Drew. You know that."

"Yeah," he said bitterly. "Well, thanks for the vote of confidence, Cindy."

She put her hand out then withdrew it just as quickly.

"I'm sorry," she whispered.

Drew ran his hands through his hair. This wasn't what he meant to talk to her about at all. He wanted to tell her he'd decided not to see her on Sunday. That it was a stupid idea … that there would be no point. And he wanted to ask her if she was still thinking about that kiss ... if she *really* meant it when she responded with such passion. But somehow they had only ended up talking about Carl and he had ended up getting angry again.

"Look," she said. "I'll see you on Sunday."

He was just about to tell her he'd decided not to go anyway when the door opened and one of her friends called out across the quadrangle.

"Cindy ... Carl's looking for you."

"Just coming." She threw him a quick, desperate glance. "Drew ... I've got to go."

Her shoulder brushed his as she walked past him and back into the college. He sat down on the wall. He leaned forward and put his hands on his knees. He stared down at his feet. Why the hell had he ended up losing his temper? It really wasn't her fault. It was him who had messed the whole thing up. The last thing he wanted was for Cindy to have a harder time than she was having already. His chest rose in a deep sigh. The stupid thing was he would have settled for her friendship if he couldn't have anything else. Life was really unfair sometimes.

He was still sitting there when Skip came out to find him.

He plonked himself next to Drew and let his hand trail in the water. "Still cheesed off?" he said without looking at him.

Drew sighed. He seemed to be doing that a lot lately. "I'm OK," he said, although he knew he couldn't fool his best friend.

"Come on." For once in his life Skip obviously

couldn't think of anything that would cheer Drew up. "I'll buy you a drink."

"Thanks." Drew got up slowly and followed Skip back inside. He knew it would take all his courage to go and face Cindy and Carl again. Luckily, when he got back in the hall they were nowhere to be seen. And, much to his relief, he didn't see them again all evening. Cindy had looked really tired. Maybe they had gone home early.

Drew spent the rest of the evening sitting dejectedly on a stool watching everyone else enjoying themselves. He felt like getting drunk but knew it would be suicide to down a few beers and then ride the bike home. He wasn't a drinker anyway. He hated the stuff. He'd tried when he was younger, like everyone else. It only made him feel lousy.

"Do you want a lift home?" he said to Marie when the disco was over. Skip had cadged a lift off someone else. They had gone into town to get a Chinese take-away.

"Yes, please," she said.

When they got home, Marie asked him in. But somehow Drew just wasn't hungry.

He shook his head. "Think I'll give it a miss tonight," he said.

She looked at him. "OK, it's up to you."

He was just about to turn the ignition back on when she said, "Remember you said we could go out together some time?"

"Yes, sure," said Drew.

Marie put her head to one side. "I don't think it's a very good idea," she said.

Drew raised his eyebrows. "Why not?"

"Well..." she fiddled with one of her dangly earrings. "I mean I really like you, Drew." She shook her head. "But the trouble is you're too much like my big brother. It just wouldn't seem right somehow."

"What you mean," he said, "is that I'm lousy company."

She put her hand on his arm. "No, Drew. It's really not that. I know we'd have a good laugh. I mean you're really good looking and lots of my friends fancy you ... it's just ... well ... you know."

Drew leaned forward and gave her a hug. "Yeah. I know, Marie. We've known each other too long."

She grinned and hugged him back. "Something like that," she said.

He kissed her cheek feeling relieved, although he never would have admitted it. It wouldn't have been fair to take her out on a date anyway. He'd only be thinking about Cindy all the time. "See you around, then, little sister," he said.

She smiled. "Yes," she said. "See you around."

8

On Saturday after work, Drew bumped into Max.

"You coming in for your work-out, Drew?" the big West Indian frowned at him. "You haven't been in for some time." He slapped Drew on the back. "Don't want you gettin' out of condition."

Drew had spotted Carl's car earlier and had made up his mind not to go to the gym that evening. "Sorry, Max," he said. "Can't make it tonight."

"Got a date?"

Drew gave him a wry grin. "I should be so lucky."

Max stared at him with a frown on his face. "Is everythin' OK at home, Drew?"

"Yes, fine. My dad's getting out soon."

"That's good." Max was still looking at him. "If ever you've got a problem you know you can talk to me."

"Thanks, Max." Drew swallowed a lump in his throat. "But everything's fine."

Drew got his jacket from the locker room and went out to the car park.

At home, he decided to have an early night. His mum had looked at him in surprise when he came through the door. She had her coat on ready to go on night shift.

"Not training tonight?" she asked.

"No." He took off his jacket and put it round the back of the chair. "I've got some studying to do." He went to the fridge and took out a can of Coke.

Mrs Devlin was looking at him. "Drew, are you all right? You look tired."

"I'm OK." He ran his hand through his hair. "College is a bit tough going at the moment, that's all."

She seemed satisfied with his answer.

"Do you want me to take you to work?" he asked.

She shook her head. "No, thanks, someone's picking me up."

He pulled the tab and took a swig of his drink. "Is Sophie in?"

"Yes, she's watching TV."

Drew said goodnight and went up to his room. He took off his clothes and lay down in his boxer shorts. He put his hands behind his head and gazed up at the ceiling. He should really be doing some studying but knew he wouldn't be able to concentrate. On one wall of the room was his dream machine poster, a Harley Davidson motorbike, gleaming purple in the Californian sunlight. He wished he could be on that bike, riding across the desert. Nothing would bother him then. Not Cindy, not his dad, not his studies ... nothing. All he would have would be the wide open spaces and freedom to do as he liked.

On the other wall was a poster of Madonna, and one of his favourite heavy metal bands. He wondered if he would really have the courage *not* to meet Cindy the following day. It seemed mean, just not turning up. He hated letting people down. Maybe he would go after all. Just to find out what she had to say. If she wanted to really talk about that kiss they had shared or if she wanted to pump him for information as Skip had suggested. It would be a good chance anyway to tell her that their friendship, such as it had been, was over once and for all. He gave a small groan. First he'd said he would meet her. Then he'd decided he wouldn't. Now, he would. He really didn't know what was the matter with him. He'd never had trouble sticking to his guns before. If this was what love did to you, then he'd be better off without it.

Through the open curtains he could see a pale moon in the twilight sky. There were some kids playing football on the green. Then he heard someone shout for them to come indoors. A car drew up outside as his mum's friend arrived to pick her up. He heard Sophie come upstairs and bang her bedroom door. Then everything went quiet.

He closed his eyes.

He must have dozed off because the next thing he knew, the phone was ringing downstairs. He sat up and rubbed his hand through his hair. He looked at his radio alarm. Eleven-thirty. Who on earth could be ringing at this time of night? Maybe it was his mum, checking that everything was OK.

He ran downstairs and picked up the receiver. "Hello?"

There was silence at the other end. That's all I need, he thought, cranky phone calls. He was just about to slam the receiver down when a voice spoke softly.

"Drew?"

His heart skipped. "Yeah ... who is it?"

"It's me," said the voice. "Cindy."

She must have looked up his number in the book.

"Cindy!" She sounded really strange. "Are you all right?"

"Yes." Her voice sounded stronger now. "I'm really sorry to bother you, Drew."

"No problem," he said. "Is anything the matter?"

"I just called to tell you I'm sorry I can't make it tomorrow."

Drew sat down, annoyed to find his legs were shaking. "Well, funnily enough, I can't either."

He was relieved when she didn't ask him why. He might not have been able to think up an excuse quick enough. "My mum's gone in for her transplant," she explained. "I've got to go to the hospital to see her."

"That's great. I really hope she'll be OK."

"Yes," Cindy said. "She's really lucky to get one so soon. I wanted to tell you earlier but you weren't in the gym tonight."

"No," he said.

"Did you have a date?"

"A date? Oh, no."

"I thought you might be meeting Marie."

"Marie?" He was surprised she knew her name. She must have asked someone. "Oh, no."

There was a small silence. Then she said, "Drew, I wanted to talk to you about Carl."

So Skip had been right. She *did* want to pump him for information.

"Cindy," he said, "we always end up talking about Carl."

"I know," she said. "But it's all tied up with what happened after the fire."

"Look, Cindy," Drew said, determined to get in first. Determined, suddenly, that she should think it didn't mean anything to him. "That kiss … it was just one of those things. We were both pretty shaken up." He really didn't know why he was saying all that. What he really wanted was to tell her he couldn't get it off his mind … that it meant more to him than anything had ever done in his life.

He waited for her to answer. Eventually she said in a stiff kind of voice, "Yes, you're right. That's what I kept thinking about. Drew, look I'm sorry Carl was such a pig to you."

"It's not your fault, Cindy. I'm grateful you rang but honestly I don't think we should be talking like this."

"No. But look, Drew … about Carl. I—"

He realized they were going round in circles. "Cindy, I'm sorry, I'm really tired and I've got a heavy day tomorrow. Let's leave it, shall we? You know he's pretty screwed up about our friendship and I think we'd better call it a day. I mean, *really* call it a day."

"Drew ... I—"

"Cindy, I've really got to go."

There was another silence. He thought he heard Cindy sniff. "OK," she said at last.

"Cindy, you were right, he really could make things rough for me. I can't afford to lose my job," explained Drew.

"I know that, Drew."

"And my dad's coming home soon. I really feel I've got enough on my plate without Hickson causing me grief."

"Yes," she said in a small voice.

"And you've got enough to cope with too. We just make trouble for each other. Cindy, it's not worth it."

If she really *was* stringing him along this would put an end to it, once and for all, thought Drew.

When there was no answer from the other end he began to think she had put the phone down. Then he heard her blow her nose and say stiffly, "OK, Drew. At least you won't be hanging around tomorrow, wasting your time."

"No," he said. "Thanks for letting me know. Bye, Cindy."

He slammed down the receiver. He leaned his head against the wall, breathing deeply. Stupid, but he really felt like bursting into tears. He'd done it, he'd really done it. He'd told her once and for all.

He sat there for a minute or two, with his eyes closed. That had got to be the most difficult thing he had ever had to do in his life.

Eventually, when he went back upstairs, it was only to lie for hours in a strange twilight world between waking and sleeping. He only finally fell into a deep sleep as the milk float came whirring down the road just before it began to get light. Even then he dreamed of Cindy. She was with Carl. They were on a yacht in the middle of a wide, blue sea. Drew was swimming towards them. But every time he looked up out of the water they had sailed further and further away.

Drew woke up the following morning feeling surprisingly better. He felt somehow as if a load had been lifted from his shoulders. Cindy knew the score now. He felt sure she wouldn't contact him again. And if they bumped into one another at college, or around the hotel? Well, he would just say "hi" like he did to anyone else and hope she couldn't tell from his face that his heart was broken.

It was the middle of the following week when Max caught up with him at work.

"Hey, Drew, come and see me when you've finished, OK?" said Max.

Drew had started training at the local sports centre. The gym there wasn't so good but at least he was managing to keep in shape. Bumping into Cindy at college he could cope with, but seeing her with Carl in the gym was a different thing entirely. He hadn't felt quite ready for that yet. He'd got the feeling that one nod in her direction might give Carl just the chance he was waiting for. He hadn't caught a glimpse of her anywhere, not at college or around the hotel. He guessed she was busy visiting her mum. He still felt mean about not explaining things to Max. So when Max asked him to call in, he agreed. He was bound to see Hickson some time … and Cindy. If they were there, so be it!

Drew finished work and went into the locker room to change. A couple of chambermaids were in there, heads together, giggling about something. They eyed Drew up and down as he came through the door. He knew these two of old. They were always chatting him up.

"Hi, Drew," the brown haired girl with a generous mouth called to him. "Haven't seen you around lately."

"Well, I've been here," he assured her. "Maybe you just weren't looking."

"Still at college then are you?" the other girl said. "Big boy like you."

Drew grinned. He used to blush every time one of the chambermaids teased him. He'd grown used to it during the couple of years he'd had the job at the hotel and now didn't bat an eyelid.

"Sure am," he said. He took his jacket and sports bag from his locker.

"You can't afford a girlfriend yet then?" the dark one said.

"That's right," Drew replied. "I prefer motorbikes anyway."

"Yes, I bet." The younger girl smiled at him.

He spread his hands. "It's true. They're a lot less trouble."

They laughed and went out, chatting between themselves. Drew put on his jacket, picked up his bag and made his way along the glass corridor to the fitness centre. Looking out, he was relieved not to see either Carl's or Cindy's car in the car park.

Max was giving a demonstration to a new customer. "Be with you in a minute, Drew," he called. "Help yourself to a drink."

Drew took a can of iced glucose drink from the cold cabinet and sat down at the counter. It was the first time he'd been there since that kiss with Cindy. However hard he tried, he still couldn't stop remembering.

"Hi," Max wiped his face on the towel slung around his neck. "How's it goin'?"

"Fine," said Drew as he felt in his pocket for a fifty pence piece for the drink.

Max waved his hand. "Have it on me."

Drew leaned an elbow on the counter. "Max, I've been meaning to talk to you."

Max eyed the sports bag at Drew's feet. "You been trainin' somewhere else?"

"Yes, that's what I wanted to explain."

Max sat down beside him. He wiped his face again. "You don't have to explain anythin' to me, Drew. You can train where you please."

"I know that, Max, but you've been really good to me and I owe you an explanation."

Max shrugged. "OK, go ahead."

Drew wasn't quite sure how it happened but he found himself telling Max the whole story. Right from start to finish ... the finish of a friendship that had never really got started.

"I feel a right coward letting Carl get to me like that," he confessed. "But I really need my job, I can't—"

"You don't have to tell me," Max said. "I know what it's like to be broke. Anyway, I reckon you did the right thing, Drew. Carl's the last person you want to be on the wrong side of ... or his father. But I'll tell you something, *you* might be fed up, but you're not the only one."

"What do you mean?" asked Drew.

"That boy Hickson's goin' round like a bear with a sore head."

"He hasn't got a sunny disposition at the best of times." Drew gave a wry grin. "You're sitting in front of an expert on the subject."

"Well I've seen him in better moods." Max shifted his massive body to try to get more comfortable on the stool. "And he and Cindy haven't been in here together for a long time."

Drew explained about her mum.

"Yeah, well, that accounts for it then. I thought maybe they'd finished," said Max.

Drew snorted. "You're joking, she's crazy about him."

"Look, Drew," Max said. "You'll get over this. There's plenty more fish in the sea. Don't waste your time longin' for somethin' you can't have."

"No." Drew finished his drink. "I don't intend to." He wished he felt as positive as he sounded.

"And come back to work-out here. Don't use that crummy gym. So what if they're in here? Show them you don't care."

"Yeah," Drew said. "Trouble is, Max, I do."

"Then pretend. Before long you'll be believin' it yourself. And find a girl ... a good lookin' guy like you, they'll be fallin' at your feet."

Drew laughed. "Careful, Max. You'll have me believing you in a minute."

"It's true, man. Take my word for it," said Max, encouragingly.

They talked for a while longer. By the time Drew left he had promised he'd come back to use the exercise machines. Max was right. He *would* show them he didn't care.

"By the way," Max said as he was going. "Are you still willin' to work here sometimes?"

"Sure," Drew said, full of new resolve. "Why not?"

"Great. I could do with you on Friday. Would you be able to make it then?"

"It'll have to be after work," he told him. Mr Appleby's got a rush job he wants me to do."

"About ten, then if that's OK," Max said. "I've promised to take Lindy to that new club in town and man will I be in trouble if I can't make it."

Drew grinned. He'd met Max's girlfriend. She was a tiny lady who ruled him with a rod of iron. "I'll come through as soon as I've finished," he said.

He made his way outside whistling. He felt better than he had for ages. His talk with Max had really done him good.

Mr Appleby was in his office. He looked up from his desk as Drew came through the door.

"Ah, Andrew," he said.

Yeah, I know, Drew thought. *I'm just the person he wants to see*.

"... just the person I wanted to see," Jim Appleby said.

The head caretaker got up and went to his filing cabinet. He took out a file and thumbed through it. Then he pulled out a piece of paper and handed it to Drew. "We've just had a delivery of three new dressing tables to replace those in these rooms."

"Right," Drew said.

"They're in the store. I want you to assemble them and take them up to the suites, OK?"

"OK," Drew said.

"Get one of the porters to help you," added Mr Appleby.

"Right." Drew took the piece of paper from him and scanned it quickly. "Are all these rooms empty?"

"Yes, but they'll be occupied from tomorrow so I want the job done tonight. If you have to put in any overtime let me know."

"OK." Drew shoved the list into his top pocket. He went out and made his way along to the store room. He would have to get a move on if he was to be finished by ten.

The job took longer than he'd thought. First he had to get all the packaging off the dressing tables. It took him half an hour to put each one together. Then when he'd done that he had to wait until one of the porters was free to help him transport them up to the rooms. It was just gone ten o'clock before he finished.

He ran along the corridor into the gym.

Max was ready to leave. He handed his set of spare keys to Drew and said goodnight. Drew had hardly time to take off his overalls when the door opened and Cindy came in.

The gym was fairly quiet. A few people were using the machines but that was all.

He heard the door go and looked up. She was standing there, gazing at him.

He swallowed quickly. "Hi," he said flatly. "Come for your work-out?" He knew it was a stupid thing to say. What else would she have come for?

"Yes." She gave him her card and he ran it through the ticket machine.

"Where's Carl?" Drew couldn't help asking.

"Er ... he's gone to a cricket club meeting or something."

"Don't you know?" Drew said bluntly. "I thought he was supposed to be your boyfriend?"

As soon as he said it, he was sorry. He saw her flinch. She was obviously going through a bad time. Her eyes were red and it didn't look as if she'd washed her hair for days. His acid remarks wouldn't help her one little bit.

She didn't reply to his comment. She just shrugged and went off to the changing room.

They didn't talk to one another any more after that. When she came out and started using the machines Drew had his head in a health and fitness magazine. He spoke now and then to customers as they went out. He changed the CD and put the pop videos into a neat pile under the counter.

It was time to close up when Cindy finally spoke to him again. She had showered and changed and was just going out of the door.

"Bye, Drew." Her eyes met his. Her hair was damp and her skin glowed from the shower. She gave him a sweet, sad smile that made his stomach turn over. "See you."

He cleared his throat. "Yeah, see you," he said softly.

He held her gaze for a while. Her lips were red, slightly parted. She looked as if she was going to say something else. He waited but she didn't. She just lowered her lashes and put her hand on the door. She pushed it open and disappeared outside.

He stared at the door for a moment. Then he sighed and turned off the CD player. He unplugged it. He cashed up, checked the money with the till receipts. Then he switched off the lights and locked up. He made his way across to the main building, gave the cash box to the night porter to put in the safe, said goodbye and left.

The car park was empty. Drew stood looking up at the stars. The night was clear. The stars were so bright it seemed as though if you stretched out your hand you might be able to touch them. The moon was silver, almost full. Somewhere, in one of the trees that bordered the riverside gardens, a nightingale sang. Drew held his breath, amazed that such a tiny creature could make such a beautiful noise. The sound brought a lump to his throat. Then, suddenly, it stopped. He waited but it didn't come again. All he could hear was a train in the distance and the sound of a jet engine way up in the night sky.

Half-way down the road towards the town centre, a Mini was parked by the kerb. He shot past before he realized it was Cindy. He had caught sight of her in his mirror. She was sitting in the driver's seat staring out of the windscreen. What on earth was she doing? Waiting for someone maybe? Well, it really wasn't any concern of his.

He drove on through the High Street. There were several people about. One or two drunks reeled in the gutter and a group of youngsters were pulling flowers from the hanging baskets outside the shopping mall. A black car passed him, then it slowed down as the driver stopped to speak to a couple of girls walking arm in arm, window shopping. He suddenly thought about Cindy again. He must have been crazy leaving her like that. She could have broken down. Run out of petrol. She might be ill, she'd certainly been under a lot of stress lately. If anything happened to her he would never forgive himself. He felt a moment of blind panic then did a rapid, rubber-burning U-turn and headed back in her direction. She might not thank him for it but he *had* to see if she was OK. He had spotted a battered white transit van parked at the junction opposite the hotel as he'd ridden out. There were two scruffy looking men in it. You never knew what kind of people were lurking about this time of the night.

To his immense relief, she was still there.

He pulled up behind the car and got off. He took off his helmet. He could still see her, just sitting there, staring into space.

He tapped on the window. "Cindy."

When she turned to him, he saw she was crying. Of course, it must be her mum. He had been so full of his own selfish thoughts he hadn't even remembered to ask how she was.

When Cindy saw him, she turned away. She began to fumble in her bag for something. He rattled the door handle. "Cindy … please."

"Go away, Drew," she shouted.

"Cindy, open the door!"

"Go away!"

He was beginning to get exasperated. "Cindy!"

She flung him a look of despair. Then she leaned across and opened the passenger door. He went round and got in.

She was still gazing straight ahead, a soggy tissue screwed up tightly in her fist.

He turned towards her. "Cindy, what's wrong?" He wanted desperately to touch her, to put his arms around her but he didn't dare.

"Nothing." She was looking in her bag for another tissue. He took his grubby, oil-stained hanky from his pocket and gave it to her.

She sniffed, then blew her nose. "Thanks." She kept it screwed up in her fist.

"Is it your mum? She's not…?"

Cindy shook her head. "No. She's not brilliant, but she's getting on OK. They say the operation should be a success."

"What is it, then?" asked Drew.

Cindy looked down, clicking her thumbnails together.

"Nothing, honestly. I just felt fed up, that's all. I'm OK, now." She tossed back her hair and looked at him. She nodded. "Really, you don't have to look like that. I'm OK."

Drew suddenly wondered if Skip had been right about something else. If she had found out about Carl's other girlfriend. He could hardly ask her, though. If she still didn't know what he was talking about he'd have really let the cat out of the bag. However much he thought she *should* know he still hated the thought of her being hurt.

"Not seeing Marie tonight?" she said suddenly.

For a second he wondered what she meant. Then he realized Cindy must really think he was going out with Marie.

"No," he said, not wanting to explain.

She was staring into space.

"Well…" He half opened the door. "If you're sure you're OK. It's not a good idea to hang around here on your own at this time of night, you know."

"No," she said flatly.

"I'll be off then." He had put one leg out on to the pavement when he felt her hand on his sleeve.

"No," she said with a kind of panic in her voice. "Don't go, Drew, please."

He turned. "Cindy, I shouldn't even *be* here. Someone might—"

"I told you," she said. "Carl's at a meeting. They were going on to a club afterwards."

"Yeah, well his dad might still be around. He was the one that caused most of the trouble last time."

"No, he won't. He and Aunty Jane were at the hospital earlier visiting Mum. They said they were going straight home. There was some old movie they wanted to watch on TV."

"It's still not a good idea," said Drew.

"Drew, I just don't want to be alone right now."

He pulled his leg back into the car. He turned his head to look at her. The glow from the overhead lamp reflected the corn-silk in her hair. She sat, not looking at him, her hands twisting themselves together in her lap making knots in his grubby hanky. She looked so unhappy that the desire to touch her, take her in his arms almost overwhelmed him. It was no good, he had to get out.

He thrust the door back open. "Cindy, I'm sorry, I've really got to go."

"Drew, please." She put her hand on his leg.

He looked down at her fingers, resting softly on his thigh. His flesh tingled. He gave a small groan, closed his eyes and rubbed his forehead. If she *was* stringing him along, then, boy, was she good at it.

She snatched her hand away. "OK," she said. "I'm sorry, I've got no right ... it's just that Dad's had to go away on business for the night and Emma's staying with a friend. I just couldn't bear the thought of going home to an empty house, that's all. I know it's stupid—"

"No," he said. "It isn't."

"Uncle John said I could go and stay there but I didn't really want to do that."

Drew wondered why not. Maybe she hadn't

wanted to lie in bed wondering what time Carl was going to get home.

"Drew," she was saying, "could we go for a coffee or something?"

He groaned again. "Cindy, that is *not* a good idea."

She sighed. "No, you're right. It isn't. Anyway there won't be anywhere open."

Suddenly he knew he just couldn't leave her, whatever the consequences. He had gone home to an empty house lots of times. When his mum was on nights and his sister was staying somewhere. He hated it too. It was a bit like going in to the *Marie Celeste*. As if the whole family had deserted you.

"I can ride back with you and see you safely indoors, if you like," he said.

She smiled and looked as if a huge weight had been lifted from her shoulders. "Drew, would you?"

"If it'll make you feel better."

"It will, honestly."

"OK, let's go." But before he could get out she put her hand on his arm.

"Drew, I'm being a real pain, I'm sorry."

"Don't keep saying sorry," he said with a grin. "I just hope your precious boyfriend isn't around, that's all."

"He won't be, I promise. The club won't shut till the early hours and he always stays until the end."

I don't know why I'm doing this, Drew thought as he followed Cindy's Mini to Manorfields. After all my resolutions not the think about her, see her, talk to her … even *care* about her. Here I am going home with her. I must be completely nuts.

Outside her house, he sat astride the bike with the engine still running. She had pulled into the drive and came back to speak to him. He took off his helmet. "I'll wait until you've gone in if you like."

"Drew, I don't suppose you'd come in for a coffee?"

"No," he said, shaking his head. "You're right, I won't."

She lowered her lashes. "OK. Thanks for coming home with me."

He watched her go down the drive to the front door. The house seemed somehow dark and forbidding. There were no lights on anywhere, not even in the front porch. At least his mum always left a light on for him if he came home late. Whether she was home or not. He suddenly realized how lonely Cindy would feel, all night in that great big house on her own. Her mum sick in hospital, her dad away somewhere. OK, so what if she *was* stringing him along. One cup of coffee wouldn't hurt. He felt all his resolutions tumble in a heap around him. He had just got to face it, being with Cindy was all he wanted.

He switched off the engine and swung his leg over the saddle. "Cindy," he called.

She turned swiftly. He propped his bike up on its stand and ran down the drive. "OK," he said, grinning. "A cup of coffee."

Her face flooded with pleasure. "Brilliant," she said. "Come on in."

* * *

Drew didn't know how long they sat talking. He only knew that when he glanced at the clock on the kitchen wall it said two-thirty. They had talked about everything. Their parents, their friends. She had told him what it was like living "down-under", her school, all the things she had dreamed of as a kid. He told her of *his* dream, to ride a Harley across the United States, on the open road.

She teased him. "You've seen too many of those old seventies movies."

"I know," he admitted. "But I still want to do it."

He told her how he felt about his father coming home. They talked about movies they had seen, music they liked, books they had read. The three hours had gone like wildfire. He had sat with her before in that kitchen. But somehow now it was different. Maybe it was because they had shared that kiss. The kiss that neither of them had mentioned even though he desperately wanted to talk about it. The memory seemed to lie between them. Silent. Unspoken. Yet undeniably there. Maybe she was too embarrassed to mention it again. Drew didn't know. All he knew was in spite of that, he felt more at ease with her than with any other girl he had ever met. He wished he could stay there for ever.

"Cindy," he said, when he had finished his third mug of coffee. "I'd really better go."

She sighed. "OK."

She stood by the door as he went out.

"You'll be OK now?" he asked.

"Yes. Thanks Drew, I'm really grateful." Her

eyes were bright in the light from the lamp. Drew let his gaze rest on her face for a moment. Then he knew, without a doubt, that he had to go, quickly, before he did something he would regret.

He put his finger out and touched her under the chin. " 'Night, Cindy," he said softly.

" 'Night," she whispered.

If she had been anyone else, looking at him like that, he might even have thought there were promises of heaven in her eyes. But as it was, she was just grateful for having had someone to talk to, someone to cheer her up when she was feeling down. He thought about Carl, out at a so-called "meeting". He must be nuts, leaving someone like Cindy on her own. Some guys didn't know when they were well off. What he did know for certain was that Skip had been wrong. She hadn't wanted to pump him for information about Carl. In fact, for a change, they hadn't even mentioned him. All she had wanted was a bit of companionship ... well, that was OK by him.

The bike engine sounded like thunder in the stillness of the warm night. His last vision of her was standing with her cheek against the door frame, watching him roar off down the road.

He was well over the speed limit going home. He didn't give it a thought. All he could think of was how good they could have been together. How deeply he could have loved her if she'd let him. How he would like to have told her, just once, how he felt. He didn't even care about Carl any more. To hell with him. To hell with his threats. If Drew did lose his job then he'd get another one. John

Hickson couldn't know *everyone* in town. He had been a fool to believe what Carl had told him.

Max had been wrong when he said he would get over Cindy. He would never get over her. Not that it really mattered. She didn't love him anyway. Never would. So what difference could it possibly make to anyone but himself?

9

The following morning Drew woke up to the sound of his mother calling to him up the stairs.

"Drew, are you awake?"

He turned over and opened his eyes. He glanced at the clock. Seven-thirty. He'd got to go to work and had only had four hours sleep. He'd be like a zombie all day. He groaned and sat up, rubbing his hands through his hair.

"Drew!" shouted Mrs Devlin.

"Yes, Mum," he yelled. "I am now!"

She came half-way up the stairs. "I'm off to work. Don't forget you promised Sophie you'd give her a lift into town."

Drew blinked. "Did I?"

She came right up and peered round his door. "Yes, she's meeting a friend at the Mall."

"I've got to go to work," he said, still blinking, still hardly knowing what day it was.

Mrs Devlin sat on the end of the bed. "Drew, you didn't get in until almost three."

"Sorry. Did I wake you up?"

"Not really. I never really settle until you're home. You know you should get more sleep if you've got all that studying to do *and* go to work as well."

Drew yawned. "Yeah, you're right." He thrust back the duvet and sat up. "Anyway, I'll drop Soph off on the way to the Pavilion. She'll have to get the bus back."

His mum stood up. "That's fine. Make sure she's got her key."

When Mrs Devlin had gone Drew lay down again. He turned over on his stomach and buried his face in the pillow. He still felt dozy. He must have woken about six times during his few hours sleep. He had no need to remind himself why. Cindy, of course. How was he ever going to get her off his brain?

Eventually, he dragged himself out of bed. He pulled a face when he saw himself in the mirror. Hair all over the place, eyes red-rimmed and bleary. A spot on his chin. What a wreck.

He shouted to his sister. "Get up, Soph, if you want a lift into town."

A voice came from downstairs. "I'm up already, aren't I?"

"Oh," he mumbled and staggered into the bathroom.

He had just finished shaving when the phone rang. Then Sophie yelled up the stairs.

"It's someone for you."

He dried his face and came out. "Who is it?"

At the foot of the stairs his sister shrugged. "I don't know. Didn't ask, did I?"

Drew swore softly under his breath. Sometimes Sophie could be a real pain. Most of the time if he really thought about it.

He ran down the stairs and into the kitchen.

"Hello?"

"Drew, it's Max." His friend sounded strange, unusually urgent and serious.

"Max! What's up?"

"Drew, can you come down here?"

"Yes, sure. Is anything wrong?"

"There's been a break in."

"Oh, no! When?"

"Last night. Look, the police are comin' and so's the boss, you'd better get down here."

"Right." Drew finished drying his face. "I'll be right there."

Sophie was leaning against the door into the sitting-room. "What's up?"

He told her. "Look, you'll have to get the bus, OK? I've got to go."

"Oh ... all right." She made a face and followed him back up the stairs and into his room.

"Do you *mind*?" he rummaged around in his drawer for a clean T-shirt. "I'm getting dressed."

Sophie pulled another face. "Well, I won't look, will I?" She went to gaze out of the window. "What's been pinched?"

"No idea." Drew pulled on his jeans and trainers. He dragged on his T-shirt and ran a comb quickly through his hair. "I'll find out when I get there."

Downstairs he grabbed an apple for breakfast. "Will you lock up and everything?" he said to Sophie.

"'Course I will. Always do, don't I?"

"Have you got enough money?" he said as an afterthought when he was half-way out of the door.

"You could lend me the bus fare if you like," she said.

Drew tutted and took a couple of pound coins from his pocket. "You owe me," he said.

"Don't I always?" She gave him one of her unexpected sunny smiles.

Drew grinned back. "Take care, now, Soph. Don't talk to any strangers."

"Get lost," she grinned again and closed the door.

The road to the hotel was busy. Roadworks along the river bridge made it half an hour before Drew arrived at the fitness centre. There was a police squad car parked beside John Hickson's Rolls and Max's jeep.

Max was standing by the counter as Drew came into the gym. His jaw dropped as he stood in the doorway. Max had said there had been a break in, but not that the place had been trashed.

"Oh, God, Max. I don't believe it."

Drew stood there looking at the mess. The potted plants had been smashed, the free weights thrown against the walls. The posters had been torn down and the drinks machine toppled over. Broken glass and mess lay everywhere. The clock had been wrenched off the wall and lay in one corner. There was a gaping hole beneath the counter where the video machine and CD player had been. The shelf that housed the TV was empty, too. Drew groaned. "They didn't have to smash the place up as well."

Max spread his hands. "Tell me about it."

It was then that Drew realized there were three other people in the room. A burly, dark-haired man in a black leather jacket. Drew knew straight away it was the police officer. And there was John Hickson and Carl. They were all staring at him.

"This is Drew Devlin," Max said. "Drew, this is Sergeant Hacker."

"Hi," Drew said. "What a mess." He wasn't scared of the police. When they came to take his father away they had been polite, kind even. He remembered the policewoman making a cup of tea and trying to comfort his mum and Sophie as they led his dad down the path.

The sergeant came towards him. "It is indeed. Max tells me you were looking after the place last night," he said.

Drew nodded. "That's right."

There was a sound from the corner and when Drew looked up, Carl was eyeing him with a frown on his face. As their eyes met, Carl leaned towards his father and said something that Drew couldn't hear. John Hickson's eyebrows shot up. "Really?" he said to Carl.

Sergeant Hacker had taken out his notebook. "What time did you leave?" he asked.

Drew shrugged. "About eleven I suppose. I'm not exactly sure."

Carl came over. He leaned one elbow on the counter and gazed at Drew. Drew felt uncomfortable. He turned. "What's so fascinating, Carl?" he asked sharply.

Carl shook his head. There was almost, but not

quite a sneer on his face. "Nothing." He nodded at Sergeant Hacker. "Go on," he said.

The sergeant raised his eyebrows, then glanced at John Hickson. "You didn't see anyone lurking about?"

Drew shook his head. "No. I locked up, took the cash tin over as usual then left. The car park was empty apart from the night porter's Fiesta."

Max butted in. "I often leave Drew to lock up for me," he said. "He uses the machines after work, sometimes quite late."

"Has he got a key?" asked Hacker.

"He's got my spare set but he always returns them to me," Max confirmed.

Drew turned to Max. "How did they get in?"

"Round the back," he said. "They smashed the cloakroom window."

"I made sure it was locked."

"Yes, they smashed the whole frame."

Drew sighed. "I'm really sorry, Max."

"It's not your fault," Max said. He turned to the sergeant. "I've got the serial numbers and everythin' of the TV and video if that's any help."

"Oh, they'll be long gone," Carl said. "You know about Devlin's father I suppose?" he went on. "You know he's in prison. Fraud, but that's only another way of saying he stole money from his firm."

Drew felt a surge of anger. Trust Hickson to bring *that* up. Before Sergeant Hacker could answer he said sharply, "What's that got to do with anything?"

Carl shrugged and went back to stand beside his father. "You tell me, Devlin."

Drew took a deep breath. "No, Carl. You tell me."

The two boys glared daggers at each other across the room. The sergeant was looking at Drew. "Any of your friends use the gym, do they, son?"

"No," Drew said. "They can't afford it. I only use it because Max lets me work-out for free."

"Hard up are they?" the sergeant said.

It didn't take much to know what he was getting at. Trust Carl to stir things up.

"Yes, as a matter of fact they are," Drew said evenly. He *had* to keep his temper. "What's that got to do with anything?"

Max put his hand on Drew's arm. "Cool it, Drew," he warned.

Sergeant Hacker was looking at his notebook. "We think the robbery took place about one-thirty," he said. He pointed to the smashed clock on the floor.

"Yeah?" Drew said. "Well I—" He stopped. One-thirty. He had been with Cindy. What if the sergeant asked where he was, who he was with?

They were waiting for him to go on.

"... I told you, I left about eleven," he said. "That's the usual time the gym closes, huh, Max?"

"Drew, you don't have to explain anythin' to me," Max said.

"No, but I'm afraid he does to me," said Sergeant Hacker.

"Yeah," Carl said. "And us."

Drew clenched his jaws together. "If you've got anything to say, Carl," he said angrily, "then say it. If you think it was me who pinched the stuff and smashed the place up, then you say so, OK?"

Carl raised his eyebrows. "If the cap fits—"

Drew lunged forward. Max stepped neatly in front of him and held his arms. "I said, cool it, Drew," he said.

Drew was shaking all over. His eyes blazed. "He can't get away with that, Max," he said through his teeth.

"Drew," Max hissed. "You're diggin' a hole for yourself, don't you see?"

Drew turned to Sergeant Hacker. "Look, if I wanted to pinch the stuff I'd have taken it out the front door, not through the window," he said.

"Yes, but that would make it rather obvious, don't you think, son?" the sergeant said. "You're a bright lad, even you must realize that."

Drew wished he would stop calling him "son".

"All right," John Hickson spoke for the first time. "Just tell the sergeant everything you know."

"I don't know anything," Drew said. He glanced desperately at Max. Surely this couldn't be happening? They couldn't really believe he'd do a thing like that.

Sergeant Hacker had been taking it all in. The hostility between the two boys, the accusing tone of Carl's voice. "Right," he said. "Now, Drew. You say you left about eleven?"

"That's right, I've told you already." Drew took a deep breath. He was beginning to calm down. He didn't even know why he was getting into such a state. He hadn't *done* anything. Max had picked up one of the stools and made him sit on it.

"Just making sure, son," Sergeant Hacker went on. "Left by yourself, did you?"

"Yes. Everyone else had gone by then."

"And you went straight home?"

Drew almost panicked. He *hadn't* gone straight home. He had gone to Cindy's. But he couldn't tell the sergeant that. Not in front of Carl and his father. Not even in private for they'd be sure to find out. He took another deep breath. "Er ... yeah," he said.

He could tell the sergeant knew he was lying. You didn't get to be a detective sergeant without having a pretty good idea when people weren't telling the truth. All he had got to do, of course, was prove it.

"You sure about that?"

"Yes," Drew said more firmly.

"So at one-thirty you were at home?"

"Yes," Drew said.

"Can anyone confirm that?"

Drew's heart sank. His mum knew exactly what time he got home. Nearer three than one-thirty. Supposing they went and asked her without her knowing why?

"Er ... no," he said.

The sergeant was looking at him shrewdly.

"There was no one at home, then."

"They were asleep," Drew said. "But I don't know why you're asking me all this. I told you, I don't know anything about it."

"He's lying," Carl said suddenly. "I can tell. Look at him, he's not even looking you in the eye."

"Shut up, Carl," his father hissed in his face. To

Drew's surprise Carl took a small step backwards. It was suddenly easy to see where he got his bullying ways from.

John Hickson nodded to Sergeant Hacker. "Go on, Sergeant."

"Now, wait a minute," Max interrupted. "Look, Mr Hacker, I trust this boy. There's no way he would have done this. What reason would he have?"

"The same reason as anyone else," Carl said. He spoke in a low voice. Almost as if he didn't want his father to hear but couldn't resist the urge to speak. "Sell the stuff ... he's pretty hard up. His mum's only a nurse and as I said, his dad's—"

Max turned. "Do yourself a favour, Carl," he said. "If you don't shut up, I'll shut you up."

Carl closed his mouth. One person he really wasn't going to argue with was Max Lewis. Drew saw a secret smile flicker around his mouth. A triumphant kind of smile. He had done exactly what he set out to do. Let suspicion fall on Drew. Drew clenched his fists together by his side. The urge to fly at Carl almost got the better of him.

The sergeant was scribbling in his book. Drew still couldn't believe this was all happening. It was like a nightmare you couldn't wake up from. He looked at Carl again, then, suddenly, he knew. This was exactly the chance Hickson had been looking for for years. The chance to get his own back for that punch on the nose. For Drew's name being linked with Cindy's. For knowing the rumours about him and the girl from Marie's school and almost getting the better of him that evening in the pub. Even if they couldn't pin the burglary on him, he had sown the seeds in his father's mind. Employing a criminal's son. He had the feeling John Hickson wasn't going to like that. He wasn't going to like it one bit. And there was only one way Drew could prove he was innocent. By telling them he was with Cindy. And that was the last thing he could possibly do.

"So there's no one," the sergeant was saying. "No one who could vouch for you?"

Drew shook his head. "No," he said. "No one."

Then, out of the blue, a voice came from the doorway.

"Yes there is. Me."

Drew spun round. Cindy was standing there. She had one hand on her hip, in the other jangled her car keys. How long she had been listening, he didn't know.

She came over and stood beside him. "I was with Drew last night, Sergeant," she said. "We were at my house. He left at gone half-past two."

Drew gazed at her in astonishment. He couldn't believe what he was hearing. She was risking her relationship with Carl to give him the alibi he needed. Could it be that she cared about him more than he'd thought? "Cindy, you don't have—"

She put her hand on his shoulder. "Yes, I do," she said softly. So softly that he thought he was the only one that could hear.

"Cindy—?"

She gave him a small, half smile. A smile that seemed to say *it's OK Drew, you don't have to worry*. Hope soared in his heart. She cared about him, she *really* cared.

Carl was standing with his mouth open. He swallowed noisily. "Cindy ... what *are* you on about?" He was almost shouting. "Why are you lying? There's no need to stick up for this creep."

She looked at him. "I'm not lying, Carl," she said. "I *was* with Drew."

Carl turned to his father. "Dad?"

John Hickson came towards them. "Are you telling the truth, Cindy?" he asked. Drew was surprised at the sudden softness of his voice.

"Yes, Uncle John," she said simply.

John Hickson turned. "That's good enough for me, Sergeant," he said. "You'll have to look elsewhere for the thugs who did this." He turned back to Drew. "Sorry, son."

Drew shrugged. He still couldn't take it all in. "No problem, sir," he mumbled.

"Come on, Carl. We're going to be late," said Mr Hickson.

But Carl was still staring at Cindy as if he had been struck by lightning.

Holding his gaze, she said with a shrug. "I'm sorry, Carl. But that's just the way it is."

Carl had gone scarlet in the face. He came and stood in front of them. "Have you been going out with him?" he asked in a low voice.

Cindy shook her head. "No."

When Drew looked at her, her face was pale and defiant. "But you've been seeing that girl from the High School," she said. "So you shouldn't complain if I spend one evening with Drew, should you?"

Drew's heart sank. So that was it. She had done

155

it just to get her own back on Carl. She probably hoped he would come to his senses and stop seeing the other girl. He should have known better than to think she really cared about him. What an idiot! He took a deep breath. Well, at least she had let him off the hook. He supposed he should be grateful for that.

Carl was breathing heavily. "You told her!" He glared at Drew. His words were like an admission of guilt.

"No," Cindy said quickly. "I got it from someone else."

John Hickson, Max and Sergeant Hacker were talking by the door.

"Carl, are you coming?" his father called impatiently. "We were supposed to be at the golf course half an hour ago."

Carl threw them one last furious look and followed his father outside.

The sergeant shut his notebook. "Well, the fingerprint boys will be here soon," he said. "Don't touch anything until they've been." He went out with Max.

"Hang on a minute," Drew called. He had suddenly remembered seeing that white transit van parked by the junction. It might be important.

When he came back Cindy was standing by the counter gazing into space. He stood watching her for a moment. She must have known he was there but she didn't look at him.

"I know why you did it," he said bluntly. He felt annoyed and angry that she had used him to get her own back at Carl. Mad at himself for being stupid enough to think there might be any other reason.

She frowned. "I don't know what you mean."

"Yes, you do." His voice came out more sharply than he had intended. "You just told Carl about last night because you'd discovered he'd been two-timing you."

She shook her head. "No, Drew, that's not true. I—"

"Yes, you did." His eyes blazed into hers. "That was probably the only reason you asked me in for a coffee ... just so you could tell Carl and make him jealous."

She looked hurt. "Drew, that's—"

But he didn't want to hear any more. "Well, thanks for getting me off the hook Cindy, but I reckon I could really have done it myself and to be honest, I don't like being used. Next time, find some other mug, huh?"

He left her standing there and stormed out. Didn't she think he had any feelings? Could she only think about herself and Carl? He knew he had to get away, to be on his own for a while. If he didn't, he might just explode.

He met Max still talking to the sergeant.

"I'll be back later to help you clear up," he said.

Max could obviously see he was angry. "I'm sorry about all that, Drew."

"It's OK, I'll get over it."

He ran out into the car park and got on his bike. He gunned the engine and sped out on to the road. He wasn't even really aware in which direction he was heading. Then he found himself approaching the bridge. He pulled up in the lay-by. He sat there for a minute, breathing heavily. Then he switched off the engine, got off, and climbed over the stile that led to the footpath along the river. Half-way, he pushed his way through the over-hanging trees and made his way along the inlet bank to the deserted boat-house. There, he sat, his knees drawn up to his chin, still trying to calm his reeling senses. How could she do it? How could she use him like that? He'd been a real fool, falling for the pleading in those big blue eyes. "I just don't want to be alone right now, Drew," she had said. No, he bet she didn't. Especially knowing that it was likely Carl was out with another girl. She hadn't needed to pump him for inform-ation because she knew already. What she had needed was a reason to really make Carl jealous. Well, he only hoped her scheme had worked.

He lay down with his face up to the sky. After a while, he felt himself beginning to calm down. So what if she had used him? It was obvious the police were going to suspect him anyway with his father and all. And John Hickson hadn't seemed to care a bit. He had even apologized. At least Carl couldn't use *that* threat against him any more. And now he knew exactly how Cindy thought of him maybe he could get on with his life.

And as for Cindy and Carl? Well, as far as he was concerned, they deserved each other!

10

It was college half-term and Drew had taken a week off work to try to catch up with his studies. By Friday, he was fed up. His mother had spent all week going round the house like a whirlwind, getting it ready for his father's homecoming. Sophie had refused to tidy her room and they had been rowing about it all week. He had tried sitting in the garden with his books but he was finding it really hard to concentrate. In the end, he gave up and phoned Skip. He hadn't seen his friend all week.

"Do you fancy going out, this evening?" he asked.

"Sure," Skip said. "Where?"

Drew shrugged. "Don't know ... just to the Mall for a pizza if you like. Everyone here's driving me mad."

They met outside the pizza place at seven-thirty. The restaurant was almost empty. It usually filled up later when everyone had finished their late-night shopping expeditions.

The waitress led them to a table for two in the corner.

"What have you been up to?" he asked Skip.

"Nothing much," Skip said. "What about you? Seen the gorgeous Cindy at all?"

Drew bit his lip. "No," he said.

"You didn't know she'd finished with Carl then?" Skip said casually taking a breadstick from its packet and biting a piece off.

Drew felt his stomach turn over. He fiddled with the paper table mat. He absent-mindedly ripped a corner off and began tearing it up into tiny pieces. It looked as if Cindy's little scheme hadn't worked after all. Instead of making him jealous it had made Carl break off the relationship. In spite of himself, he felt a pang of sorrow. She had really loved that guy and now it seemed he didn't want her. He knew exactly how she felt.

"Oh?" he said, trying to sound as if it didn't really matter to him *what* Cindy was up to. "I knew she'd found out about the other girl." He went on to tell Skip what had happened at the gym.

"Well, that finished it then, I reckon," Skip said.

"How do you know anyway?" asked Drew.

"I saw her."

"Where?"

"At the hospital. My grandad's gone in for a check-up. Something to do with his heart. I met her on the way out."

"Oh," Drew said. "Her mum's still in there, then?"

"Looks like it." The waitress came over to take their order. When she had gone, Skip said, "She asked how you were."

"Yeah? I'm surprised she's interested," said Drew.

Skip leaned forward. "Drew, she looked really fed up."

"Did she?"

"Yes. Look, there's nothing to stop you asking her out now. That's if you still fancy her."

Drew snorted. "She wouldn't go out with me if I was the last guy in the universe."

"That's not the impression I got."

Drew glanced up at his friend. "What do you mean?"

"She said she'd really like to see you, to explain things. I didn't know what she meant at the time but I guess I do now."

"Yeah," Drew said bitterly. "I bet she would." Then he added quickly. "Why didn't you tell me this before?"

Skip sat back again. "She asked me not to. She thought if you wanted to see her you'd get in touch."

Drew shrugged. "Yeah, but if she *really* wanted to get together, she'd ring *me*, wouldn't she?"

"I suppose so. Although if you looked as mad then as you do now, then she probably thinks you'll have a go at her."

"Yeah, well I probably would. She can say what she likes but I still think she used me to get back at Carl." Drew didn't want to talk about her any more. "Look, Skip, let's change the subject shall we? How's Marie?"

"Marie? She's OK," Skip grinned. "She's got a boyfriend. Someone in the sixth form."

"Oh?" Drew raised his eyebrows. "What's he like?"

"Oh … tall and spotty with long hair. A bit like you were at that age."

Drew managed a smile. "Thanks very much."

Drew didn't enjoy his pizza. All he could think of was what Skip had told him about Cindy and Carl. Once or twice he realized his friend was talking to him and he hadn't heard a word he had said. Cindy and Carl … finished. A few weeks ago he would have been over the moon. Now, knowing she was unhappy just made him feel more miserable than ever.

In the end, Skip gave up trying to make conversation. They finished their meal in silence.

"Look, old pal," Skip said as they were walking towards the car park, "go and see Cindy … get things sorted. You can't go around being a drag for ever."

"There's nothing to sort," Drew said.

"You know it's not like me to admit I'm wrong," Skip said looking serious. "But I take back all I said about Cindy. I honestly don't think she *was* stringing you along at all. She gave me the impression she really cared about you. Just get in touch with her, it won't do any harm."

On his way home, Drew stopped off by the river. He seemed to be spending a lot of time there lately. He reckoned things would still probably be bedlam at home and he needed to think.

The roadworks had extended right across the

bridge now so he wheeled his bike a little way along the footpath. He left it propped up behind a tree. It was probably safer there anyway. than in full view of passing traffic.

It was a sultry evening, the air heavy and still. Mosquitoes danced over the water and the ducks swam languidly in the slowly moving current.

Drew walked along the footpath and threaded his way through the trees to the old boat-house. Last time he had been there it had been after the break-in. He had been confused then. He was even more confused now. It seemed likely he would stay that way for a long time to come.

He took off his jacket and sat down on the bank. The water seemed to calm him. It was always the same down here. The stillness, the beauty ... it put your problems into perspective. Even from here, though, you could still hear the noise of the rush-hour traffic across the bridge. It was like the distant thunder of a slowly departing storm. It seemed as if it was there to remind you there was a real world outside. One you had to go back and face whether you liked it or not. He thought of all those wide open spaces he longed to travel. One day, Dev, he said to himself. One day. Maybe that would be the answer. To get away ... really get away. Away from Cindy ... everything. A few more terms at college then he would be free. He wondered how his father had not been driven mad. He might have been in an open prison but it was a prison just the same. You don't always need high brick walls to deny you your freedom.

Suddenly Drew heard a soft sound. The hiss and

swish of someone walking through the grass. He swore softly under his breath. Some fisherman, he guessed, come to disturb his peace.

But it wasn't a fisherman. It was Cindy. When she saw him sitting there she gave a small gasp of surprise.

"Drew!"

He was so stunned he couldn't speak. It was almost as if, just by thinking about her, he had willed her to be there.

She looked embarrassed. "Look, I'm sorry. I didn't know you were here. I didn't see your bike."

He told her where he had left it.

"Right, well, I'll go." She made a small gesture with her hands. "I don't want to disturb you."

But he couldn't let her just disappear like that. He leapt to his feet. "No, Cindy, wait. Please don't go."

She came and sat beside him. A little way away, not so close that their shoulders touched. They sat in silence, knees drawn up, looking out over the water.

He glanced at her from under his lashes. She wore white jeans and a blue sweatshirt that brought out the colour of her eyes. Her hair was loose, falling softly over her shoulders. He swallowed. "Er ... I heard about you and Carl," he said eventually.

"Skip told you I suppose." She didn't look at him.

"Yes. Your plan didn't work, then?" He couldn't help it, he still felt convinced she had used him.

She glanced at him sideways. "I never had any plan, Drew."

He snorted. "Pull the other one. You used me against Carl. You told Hacker you were with me the night of the robbery to make Carl jealous."

He picked a blade of grass and stuck it between his front teeth, biting down on it hard. Its bitterness seemed to reflect his mood.

"Drew... I..." she began.

"Don't give me that, Cindy," he interrupted. "I know exactly what—"

Suddenly she turned on him. Her eyes were burning with anger. "Shut up, Drew!" She turned away again and put her hands over her face. "Just shut up, will you!"

He had never seen her angry before. Not really angry. So furious that she began to cry. In spite of everything, his heart turned over. He put out his hand then snatched it back quickly. God, what a fool he was. He'd blown it again.

"I'm sorry," he said hastily. "I—"

"So you should be!" She was shaking with rage. "I don't understand you. Why won't you listen to me? You keep saying you're sorry then you carry on being the same as ever."

Without looking, she thrust out her arm and pushed him in the chest. Hard. Surprised, he fell backwards.

She jumped to her feet. "You must be completely blind if you can't see why I told them," she shouted, wiping the tears angrily from her face.

He leapt to his feet beside her. "OK, then!" He was shouting now. They were both breathing heavily, eyes blazing at one another. "Tell me!"

He waited for her to speak. His nostrils flared,

his chest rising and falling rapidly. "Come on," he urged when she didn't seem to be able to find the right words. "Spit it out!"

The air between them seemed to drum with the beating of his heart.

The anger left her face as quickly as it had come. She raised her hands then let them fall to her sides. "Oh," she said hopelessly. "What's the use."

She turned and walked away.

In one bound he was beside her, holding her arms, spinning her round to face him.

"Tell me, Cindy!" he demanded.

She stepped back, away from him. It was as if she wouldn't be able to think straight if he was still touching her.

And so at last he let her explain.

"I told them because it was true," she said. "And because I didn't care who knew we had been together."

He swallowed. "Even if…"

"Yes, even if it meant Carl finished with me." She gazed at him, her eyes still swimming. "Drew, have you any idea what I felt when you kissed me that night?"

He shook his head, dumbstruck. "No … I only know…"

She lifted her shoulders. "Drew, I couldn't get it out of my mind. No one in my life has ever kissed me like that before. I couldn't stop thinking about it. I wanted to tell you so much…" Her voice broke.

He put his hand out and touched her arm. "Cindy?"

She cleared her throat noisily. "Drew, I think about you all the time. How we get on so well together. How you make me laugh." She sniffed and wiped the back of her hand across her nose. "I tried to tell Carl that maybe we should end our relationship. He's as bad as you, Drew. He just *wouldn't* listen to me. Then I saw you with Marie and I realized you only thought of me as a friend."

Drew groaned and tried to say something. She waved her hand, shaming him into silence.

"Then you said that kiss didn't mean anything and I thought it was hopeless. And another thing … I knew how upset Mum and Dad would be if I split with Carl. I didn't want to cause them any more stress. I was scared of my feelings for you, Drew." Her mouth quivered. "I knew if Carl found out he would make life hell for you. But somehow, however hard I tried to tell myself I should forget you, nothing made any difference."

"Oh, Cindy," Drew groaned again and shook his head. He could hardly believe what he was hearing.

"I think Carl knew," she said. "That's why he was so paranoid about our friendship. He must have seen something that I couldn't see myself."

"Cindy—" Drew tried to speak.

"… and then someone told me Carl was seeing someone else," she went on, her voice breaking again. "You know what, Drew? I didn't care. I just didn't care. All I could think about was you." She sniffed. "And the evening of the break in … after we'd talked and you had been so good at cheering me up, I knew I couldn't go on seeing Carl. I knew I only wanted you. I made up my mind to tell him once and for all. I'd hardly seen him all week anyway so I phoned first thing in the morning. Aunty Jane told me he and Uncle John had gone to the fitness centre so I went to find him. That's when I heard Carl trying to pin the robbery on you." Her face crumpled and she began to cry again. "I tried to explain," she sobbed. "You just wouldn't give me the chance."

Drew ran his hands through his hair. It was as if all his nightmares had suddenly turned to dreams. "You really care that much about me?" he whispered.

She wiped her face on the corner of her sweatshirt. He was gazing at her speechlessly. The anger had gone from her eyes and all he could see was love.

"What do *you* think?" she said simply.

He held out his arms. "Cindy … come here."

She came to him then. She put her arms round his waist and laid her head softly against his chest. Then she put her fingertip up and touched his face gently. "Can't you see, you stupid idiot," she murmured. "I *love* you."

Her arms went up round his neck. He could feel her crying softly into his shoulder. He held her gently. He was shaking all over, his mind a whirl of emotions. He could still hardly believe what she had said.

She loved him … him … him. Her words seemed to sing and soar around him like the song of the nightingale that had touched his heart.

She lifted her face to his and he kissed her. Softly at first, his mouth trembling against hers.

Then she pulled him closer and was kissing him as if her life depended upon it. Wild, quick kisses that sent fire through his veins and made his heart sing with joy.

Eventually, he had to push her away. He smiled into the blueness of her eyes. "Hey, Cindy," he said breathlessly. "Give me a break, will you."

"Oh, Drew," she breathed. "You're such a fool."

"I'm sorry," was all he could say. She was right. He was a fool, a stupid, blind, dumb, impatient fool.

"It's OK," she was murmuring, kissing him again. "Everything's OK, now."

Eventually she drew away. "What about Marie?" she said suddenly.

"She never was my girlfriend. I suppose I let you think that on purpose." He touched her face, her hair. He ran his shaking fingertip round the line of her jaw. His eyes went round her face. "I love *you*, Cindy. More than I've ever loved anyone in my life."

She hugged him so tightly it seemed she wanted to get right inside his skin.

"I thought," she said, "when you kissed me that night that maybe you loved me too. But then you said it was just one of those things. I wasn't sure."

"I was," he said. "I was always sure."

They stayed there until it was dark. Sitting close, heads together, fingers, arms entwined.

"I talked it over with my Mum," Cindy told him. "She was upset about me and Carl but she said I should be with the person I want to be with, no one else."

"She's pretty sensible, your mum."

"Yes." She held his hand against her cheek. "I guess she is."

He turned and kissed her hair. Letting his mouth rest there, feeling the silk against his face. It smelt of herbs and flowers. When she smiled at him, her eyes were full of promises of heaven. And he knew, without a shadow of doubt, that the promises were all for him.

All the problems they might have to face suddenly came crashing in on him. *She* might not mind about his father but her parents might have different ideas. And there was still Carl to contend with. He had a feeling their quarrel wasn't over by any means.

"It's not going to be easy, you know," he murmured. "My dad and everything ... your parents aren't going to like it one bit. Then there's Carl..."

She touched his face. "I don't care." She snuggled into the warm circle of his arms. "All I care about is you."

And Drew realized that he didn't care either. With Cindy beside him he could face anything.

He felt a moment of perfect peace.

They were together ... his love was no longer a secret.

Nothing else mattered.

"No," he murmured. "Come to think of it, neither do I."